THE STONE BOY

Sophie Loubière

Translated from the French by Nora Mahony

TRAPDOOR

First published in France by Univers Poche in 2011
under the title *L'Enfant aux Cailloux*
First published in Great Britain in 2013 by Trapdoor
This paperback edition published in 2014 by Trapdoor

A CIP catalogue record for this book
is available from the British Library.

ISBN 978-1-8474-4583-4

Printed and bound in Great Britain by
Clays Ltd, St Ives plc

Papers used by Trapdoor are from well-managed forests
and other responsible sources.

MIX
Paper from
responsible sources
FSC® C104740

Trapdoor
An imprint of
Little, Brown Book Group
100 Victoria Embankment
London EC4Y 0DY

An Hachette UK Company
www.hachette.co.uk

www.littlebrown.co.uk

D

HACKNEY LIBRARY SERVICES

Please return this book to any library in Hackney, on or before the
last date stamped. Fines may be charged if it is late. Avoid fines by
renewing the book (subject to it NOT being reserved).

Call the renewals line on 020 8356 2539

3/14

People who are over 60, under 18 or registered disabled
are not charged fines.

0 4 NOV 2016		
- 9 JUN 2017		

(-) Hackney

To my mother,
a woman of courage and tragedies.

It is better to save a guilty man
than to condemn an innocent one.

VOLTAIRE, *Zadig*, or, *The Book of Fate*

LIVING UP
TO EXPECTATIONS

'Each of us has heaven and hell in him ...'

OSCAR WILDE, *The Picture of Dorian Gray*

1

July 1946

The sun and wind were playing a lively game with the curtains. The little boy smiled up from his chair. To him it seemed like an invisible creature being tickled by this summer Sunday, playing hide-and-seek behind the jacquard fabric. When he closed his eyes, the child would have sworn that he heard chuckles of delight underneath the medallion print.

'Gérard!'

With his back straight and his palms either side of his plate, the little boy turned to look out of the window onto the garden. A glorious scent emerged from bunches of gladioli, lilies and dahlias. Their astonishing colours sent bursts of light into the half-lit room. Peas rolled into the chicken gravy, swept aside by knife blades, indifferent to the lunchtime conversation.

Gérard went back to chewing, his nose in the air, hammering kicks against the legs of his chair. He wasn't remotely interested in the subjects raised by his uncle, parents and grandparents – wage claims brought on by a rise in food prices, the 'teeny-tiniest swimsuits in the world', an American nuclear test done on the Bikini Atoll in the Pacific and a trial in Nuremberg.

'Goering is pleading not guilty. It makes your blood run cold.'

Gérard's uncle passed the silver breadbasket to his neighbour.

'The defendants don't feel responsible for the crimes of which they've been accused,' exclaimed Gérard's father before biting down on a crouton.

The little boy had turned his chicken skin into little balls and pushed it into his cheeks, and now raised a white napkin to his lips, pretending to wipe his mouth, and slyly spat out the chewed meat. All Gérard had to do then was drop the napkin under the table. Like every Sunday since the end of the war, the cat would come later to erase all trace of his crime. But then, something disturbed the natural order of things. A voice rose across the crystal glasses.

'Daddy, last night I saw Mummy.'

Sitting stock still at her place with her back to the window, Gérard's cousin smiled. Everyone's gaze converged on the little girl with the thick hair cut short below her ears. A dark fringe stopped at her eyebrows, and her emerald-green eyes shone out below.

'She came into my room and sat down on the bed.'

Gérard froze. A breeze lifted the curtains, giving everyone at the table the shivers. His uncle blotted his moustache with the corner of a napkin.

'Elsa, be quiet, please.'

'You know what? She was wearing her flowered dress. The one you like so much, Daddy.'

His grandmother let out a moan and waved a hand in front of her face as if to chase away flies.

'Elsa, go to your room,' insisted her father.

The little girl's face was as pale as a bar of soap.

'She said you shouldn't worry about her. Mummy is well. She says she sends you a kiss. All of you. You too, Gérard. But she doesn't want her nephew to feed the cat under the table any more, she says it's disgusting.'

Gérard dropped his napkin. The contents shook out across his shorts, revealing his attempted sleight of hand. In the same instant, a slap stung his left cheek.

'I told you to stop that!' his mother scolded.

Tears filled the little boy's eyes and his stomach hurt. He lowered his head towards his stained shorts, so he didn't see his uncle get up from the table and haul his daughter unceremoniously off to her room. Elsa's cries echoed in the stairwell. No one dared eat dessert. The St Honoré cake stayed wrapped in its paper, much to the chagrin of Gérard, who was being pushed out onto the landing by his mother before he could even button his waistcoat.

'Would you hurry up? Stop dawdling!'

Gérard hated his cousin since she had gone crazy.

They don't believe that you're alive, but they're wrong.
All I have to do is close my eyes to find you.
You're wearing your pretty dress covered in flowers
And you've tied a scarf in your hair too quickly.
I think that you're kissing me, crying.
My cheeks smell of your kisses.
You walk so quickly that the train has already carried
  you away.
You're going to come back. I'm certain that you're going
  to come back.
It's only a name on a list.
Daddy's wrong.
They're all wrong.

2

August 1959

The young man slowly locked his arms across Elsa's chest. He held her tightly against his body, not letting go. Her eyes closed, the young girl kept her mouth open, as if she were at the dentist. She breathed like a puppy that had run about too much, her head bent back, inflating her gingham blouse. A sigh escaped her lips.

'Go ahead. Squeeze. Squeeze me tight, cousin.'

In Elsa's garden, between the cherry tree and the chaise longue missing its cushion, Gérard felt confused. An overpowering sensation emanated from the young girl and her surroundings. The lawn seemed to be inhaling the young man feet first, the plum trees bending towards Elsa, holding out their ripe fruit. When he was with his cousin, the world seemed to shrink around her and her alone, erasing everything around them, leaving just the faintest outlines; Gérard could only make out the beauty of this incandescent girl as he swooned.

'The stars,' she said, her voice barely audible. 'I can see tiny yellow stars. Squeeze again!'

Gérard's arms tensed, responding to the plea in spite of himself. Then, suddenly, the gasping stopped. She collapsed. Her body slid against her cousin's stomach and fell to the ground like a sack of laundry. The young man rushed to hoist her onto the chaise longue. He slapped lightly at her cheeks, moaned her name and felt for her pulse, but he couldn't manage to find it in her ivory-coloured wrist.

'Elsa? Elsa!'

He brought his mouth to her lips to give her some air. There was no sign of life. Sobbing, he shook the young woman by the shoulders.

'Elsa! Answer me!'

He cursed himself for surrendering to the young girl's capricious desires, for agreeing to play such an idiotic game with her, gambling her life for a thrill. But he hadn't wanted to look weak in front of Elsa, so he had slipped his arms under hers and squeezed and squeezed.

'Elsa, please!'

As Gérard had often witnessed before, his cousin made a miraculous return from the dead with a cosy laugh, coughing, like a little girl recovering from being tickled.

Toughened up by her years at boarding school, she had no doubt fraternised with girls – girls from good families – and broken the rules of her orderly upbringing. Elsa had snuck out and developed a taste for the forbidden, but there was nonetheless a casual grace about her, and she was as confident as a boy.

'It was delicious, cousin.'

Elsa grabbed Gérard by his shirt collar and pulled their mouths together.

'Do it again. Suffocate me in your arms. Make me die again.'

The touch of madness was irresistible.

Saint-Prayel School, Moyenmoutier
15 September 1961

Dear Daddy,

The students in my class are horribly clever, regardless of how Mr Mohr goes on about them. I'm grateful to them for making my job easier for me: I'm much encouraged by my first steps on the path to teaching. I believe that children have things to teach us about our capacity for understanding and grasping the truths of this world. They hide behind new words, ones they've barely learned, and I find it endearing.

I miss you, and the house, too. Here, I often go for walks. The forests are magnificent and I breathe in pure air that smells of ferns. Mummy would find the region too cool, though.

I have a comfortable little apartment just above the school that comes with the job, but I am fairly isolated and far from the town. Gérard doesn't visit me unless he gets leave, which is rare. In Algeria he is mainly treating civilians, and tells me he is performing amputations on children. I think that the Algerians aren't just fighting for their independence; they're starting a real revolution. It's all anyone talks about around here. Sons, husbands — many of the men have left, and those who come back are demoralised or violent. They've all become hardened, and they put on an arrogant machismo. They have to learn to respect their wives and children again. Some have come back so burdened that they are physically hunched over, their shirtsleeves sticking out from under their jackets, as if they were carrying stones in their hands.

Forgive me for writing about sad things again, but I have no one to tell other than a stray dog who pisses against my door. I chase him out of the playground regularly, as I don't want him to give the children rabies. I hope that you're well and that you don't miss me too much.

With love and kisses,
Elsa

3

She was standing up in her room a metre away from her bed, staring at the ceiling. There was an odd noise, like a marble rolling along the floorboards. The noise stopped, and started again, this time like the shoes of a dancer called to the attic for a macabre ballet. The woman stood in the middle of the room, dressed in a nightgown, one hand sliding beneath her round belly.

Leave me alone. Leave me alone, please.

She had got up to drink a glass of water to improve her circulation. Then, when she was back in her room, she opened the curtains, worried. With her face tilted towards the frost-covered glass, she looked out beyond the chestnut tree, looking around for someone, a shadow crossing the snowy garden, the memory of a floral dress disappearing around the corner of the street one spring day during the war. Then the noise happened again. A marble across the floor. Sashaying footsteps.

No. I'm begging you. Go away!

Elsa was standing still by the window, her skin taking on a bluish cast from the street lamp. Her knees weakened and buckled, and she writhed in pain. Overhead, the noises started again, louder, in the rhythm of her contractions with each pitch and roll of her insides. She didn't groan, didn't scream, didn't wake her husband.

Leave me alone! I don't want to come with you! Not now!

It was two hours since the sun had withdrawn from her frozen feet. The noise of her fall had woken Gérard. His young wife was sitting in a puddle of blood. Elsa was giving birth.

22 August 1974

Gérard,

*I can't go on with your way of life any more. Your
absences are longer than ever. Seeing you come back
late, neglecting your son and your wife, all so that
you can take care of people other than us – people
who aren't suffering like I am – is not acceptable. To
endure the weariness of a doctor who has reached his
limit, to be subjected to your mood swings and your
listlessness, is too much for me. I already know the
scene, there's no need to play it out further. Your plan
to leave for Canada to take up your studies again and
to specialise is a shining example of your egotism.
How can you intend to dedicate your life to diseases
of the heart when you show so little regard for my
heart and that of your son? Did you even think of us,
of what I would be obliged to sacrifice in order to
follow you – my position as headmistress, for
example?*

I would prefer that you not return home again and

17

that, in time, you rent a studio so that you can take stock of the situation.

This changes nothing about my feelings for you. I love you; you are the only man in my life and my son's father.

I will take care of explaining the situation to Martin.

Elsa

4

Kneeling in front of the low table in the living room, the child unwrapped his present with the enthusiasm of a man condemned to death. The size of the item covered in forest-green paper was far too modest to correspond to Martin's hopes. He had asked for a giant Meccano set and a chemistry kit for his birthday. The child held up the package: too heavy for a board game or a giant puzzle.

'Go ahead, Martin, open your present.'

His mother forced a smile through too much make-up. Her lipstick was like a dark purple train track through the snow. The cider was too sharp and the chocolate cake needed more butter. Also wanting were Martin's class-mates: the little party couldn't be held until the second

Wednesday in January. There was no upside to being born between Christmas and New Year at all. It was usually impossible to get all of your friends together, the luckier of whom had gone skiing, and there was the dis-appointment of Christmas gifts being put aside for your birthday 'unless your parents thought ahead', which was never the case with Martin's parents. So, the gifts that he received were rarely as impressive as those opened by his friends twice each year. Regardless, Martin's mother had always held on to the idea that they should 'mark the occasion'.

'A little party, just us. What do you say?'

Sitting on the big armchair in the living room, her knees together below her lilac wool dress, she looked like she was praying, her elbows bent, watching Martin's fin-gers tear open the wrapping paper on his first gift. When he saw the encyclopaedia, the child turned pale.

'Do you like it?'

'It's not what I wanted.'

'It's a useful gift. You'll need it for your studies.'

'Yes, but it's not what I wanted.'

'We don't always get what we want in life, Martin. Open your other gift.'

'If it's like the first one, I don't want it.'

'Stop that. Go on, open it. It came from Galeries Lafayette in Paris.'

Martin pulled off the paper more quickly this time:

maybe it was one of those wonderful toys he'd seen last week in the window of the big Parisian shop. Inside a grey cardboard box lined in cellophane, the little boy found a pair of mittens and a matching hat.

'It's pure wool. You won't be numb with the cold going to school in the morning with them.'

The hat was rust-coloured with brown snowflakes embroidered on it. It was a ridiculous thing to put on in the playground. Martin looked at his mother, incredulous.

'Why did you buy me that?'

She leaned down to her son and caressed his face.

'Listen, Martin, times are hard, as well you know. Your father has abandoned us and I have to get by on just my own salary, so—'

'That's not true! You're talking rubbish!'

On the verge of tears, Martin threw the box and its contents on the ground, then ran out and shut himself in his room. His mother's voice echoed up the stairs: 'Come now, try to be reasonable, Martin! You need a hat much more than a Meccano set!'

2 April 1979

For the attention of the Director of the County Council
of Seine-Saint-Denis

Sir,

*Allow me to bring your attention to a sect that appears to
be operating currently in Seine-Saint-Denis and with
which I have unfortunately been in contact several times
following a family tragedy.*

*This organisation pretends to heal psychological
damage and serious illness through nutrition and
extreme fasting. Without a doubt, it involves cult-like
behaviour.*

*I had the opportunity to test several of their methods,
including instincto-therapy, and I can report that the
kind of practices suggested reduce the patient to an
extremely fragile mental state. They allow the patient to
become enthralled by what they are devoting themselves
to, sometimes causing social and family breakdown in*

22

cases where these were not the original causes of the patient's isolation.

Certain individuals call themselves shamans, but they are nothing but frauds. That is the case for the person whose name and address is attached herewith. He is currently offering wildly expensive weekends at his farm in Neufmoutiers-en-Brie, where they are holding seminars on Peru on the pretext of helping his followers to reach, and I quote, 'a quest for a redeeming self truth'. I think that this person is a crook. Personally, I have given him a great deal of money, thinking that he would help my father to overcome his cancer. Result: my father had a brutal relapse due to a massive vitamin B deficiency. I have already filed a report with social services and at the police station in my town, but the man is well established here and gains new followers daily in market squares across the region — that's where he's based, behind the counter at his supposedly organic fruit and vegetable stall.

Dreadful charlatans are hiding behind this façade of getting back to nature and alternative psychology. We cannot allow not only a great many adults, but their children, too, to be subjected to such danger. As the headmistress of a school, I know certain parents who are in thrall to this gentleman, and who swear by him and him alone to heal their families. I could not let such instances with medical and social implications go unreported.

I am depending upon your swift intervention in this matter.

Yours faithfully, with respect,

Mrs Elsa Préau
Headmistress of Blaise Pascal School

PS: I have CCed this letter to the Minister of Health and the Police Commissioner.

5

On the third floor of the hospital complex in Seine-Saint-Denis, an overweight female doctor was sitting in a narrow room behind a desk groaning with files. She was speaking to Mrs Préau, and Mrs Préau was listening to her as closely as she could, her hands folded and her legs crossed. She had the distinct feeling that other people were standing around her – medical personnel, nurses, orderlies with mocking expressions. The woman in the white blouse was explaining something very important. It was precisely for this reason that there were so many people in this room staring at her.

'The battle is over, Mrs Préau. What you have done for your father all these years is outstanding. You have managed to keep him in the best possible physical condition, well beyond the prognosis that we gave him after his remission.'

What was worrying Mrs Préau was her ability to take in what this pink-cheeked woman was going to tell her. These past years had been difficult, and her nerves were frayed. Martin's departure for Canada hadn't helped things. But she understood that her son's studies took precedence over his mother and that he needed to be closer to his father.

'I understand that it is difficult to hear this, but I know that you can take it. If we look at the MRI . . . '

Mrs Préau turned towards the window and concentrated on the view of the park. Poplars quivered in the rays of the setting sun. It would be so lovely to walk along there just now, and leave behind this sentencing.

'Overall, his health has deteriorated. We will give him the best possible care, but you should know that he will continue to suffer.'

Her mother would have so loved those pathways of white flowers, the foliage turning inky in the shadow of the beech trees. Mrs Préau would take her father there twice a week, pushing the wheelchair to a bench where, in the shade of a honeysuckle, she would sit, the invalid by her side. She would read the paper to her father, commenting passionately about the first measures put in place by the new government – measures that would give the

French people a more optimistic perspective about their future.

'If he were to fall victim to respiratory failure, we need your authorisation – do you understand?'

The new government didn't waste any time: raising the minimum wage, increasing the minimum rate for the old age pension and child benefits, temporarily suspending the deportation of foreigners . . . And then there was that astonishing festival dreamed up by the Ministry for Culture, a national day dedicated to music! Mrs Préau asked suddenly:

'What is the date today?'

'The twenty-first of June.'

'Yes, of course. Where is my head—'

'Mrs Préau, do you give us your consent so that we could let him *go*?'

At the school today, they were celebrating the first day of summer in the playground. Mrs Préau had arranged for break time to be livened up for the children with songs and dancing. A tiring day. They hadn't heard shouts of joy like that since the last school fête. The head-mistress's heart was still swelling with happiness.

'Mrs Préau, please, we need your consent.'

The ill man's daughter turned to face the doctor and noticed her hostile expression. Pink and white scrubs moved back and forth behind her restlessly, sharpening their syringes.

'Tell me, Doctor,' whispered Mrs Préau, 'this evening, for the music festival, couldn't you just see your devoted orderlies singing the latest hits to the patients just before they gave them the lethal injection?'

13 March 1997

Audrette,

*I am sorry to have to write you this letter, but you have
given me no choice.*

*You cannot get away with it just because you're my
daughter-in-law. Refusing to let me see my grandson is
enormously cruel. I do not see how his spending
Wednesday afternoons with his granny poses such a
problem for you. Bastien is a charming child, he's very
intelligent, and he's my only grandchild. I'm also very
concerned about his health; Bastien has lots of bruises.
Does he have trouble with his balance? Does he fall
often? If not, do you see any reason for his contusions?*

*I think that you are being subjected to a bad influence
at the moment, one that is altering your perception of
things. I have another hypothesis about your situation,
but I would rather discuss it face to face. And I don't see
how keeping a goat and a baboon in my garden could
possibly be harmful to my grandson. On the contrary; it
has been proven that contact with animals is particularly*

beneficial to children. Besides, Bamboo never gets out of his cage.

I should warn you, however, that if you prevent me from seeing Bastien, I will be obliged to contact the judge at family court. I intend to exercise my visitation rights just like any other grandmother.

Kiss Bastien and Martin for me.

Elsa Préau

6

The scrawny daisies had been pulled up by the root. The dandelions, too. Parched by the heat, the earth crumbled between your fingers.

'Are they for me, Bastien?' asked Mrs Préau.

'No, they're for Mummy.'

The little boy held the makeshift bouquet tightly in his left hand. He walked with his head bobbing, one palm against his granny's, which was damp with sweat. There wasn't a breath of wind to chase the dog days of summer away.

'I really like Captain Cousteau.'

'Me too, Bastien.'

'Why did he die?'

'Because the Good Lord needed him.'

'It's not fair. Who's going to take care of the whales now?'

'You, when you're older.'

'Granny Elsa?'

'Yes, Bastien?'

'Why did you come to school to pick me up and not Mummy?'

'Because she had to work. She'll come later.'

On the path, between two verges of yellow grass that had grown up beneath the tarmac, a colony of fireflies had caught the child's eye. He stopped for a moment to watch the insects mating happily.

'What kind of insects are these, Granny Elsa?'

Mrs Préau raised an eyebrow.

'Not God's creatures, certainly.'

'Oh?'

'Come on, Bastien, let's cross.'

'But that's not the way home.'

'We're not going home. We're going to have a picnic in Courbet Park with our after-school snack.'

'Great!'

'I made chocolate cake.'

The little boy's face lit up. He readjusted one of the straps of his schoolbag and pulled at the elastic of his shorts before stepping out onto the zebra crossing.

Twenty minutes later, Mrs Préau and her grandson were picnicking on the grass in the shade of the big chestnut trees. Bastien made a face. He put what was left of his cake down on a paper napkin.

'I don't feel good, Granny.'

He ran his hand through his hair.

'Did you eat too quickly?'

'No, I'm dizzy.'

She put a hand to his burning forehead.

'I told you not to stay on the swing for too long in the sun. Have some juice.'

Bastien drank straight from the plastic bottle. Soon he was sleeping, his cheek pressed against his granny's skirt, listening to a story about goblins.

'... they wore hats as tall as they were wide and big belts made of wolf skin across their black woollen coats. Everyone in the village was afraid of their nasty tricks. They were the ones who would drop things in the middle of the night, or make the floorboards creak in people's houses. They could open any door. No lock could keep them out. They were so ugly that when women saw them, they would faint from fright. Even the strongest men and the bravest children would take to their heels when they crossed paths with a goblin.'

Bastien's grandmother brought the last piece of cake to her lips. Her arm was shaking gently, trailing crumbs across her blouse.

'They were very nasty goblins sent by the County Council. The same ones who spoke to your lovely mummy in her sleep, all the better to manipulate her, and to make her do very nasty things to her family, and most of all to you, my little Bastien.'

Nodding off, the grandmother closed her eyes too.

'But you, my dear, they'll never have you. Your granny won't let her grandson be part of anything wicked. No one will lay a finger on any blood of mine. Sleep, my Bastien, sleep tight. Granny Elsa is watching over you . . . '

Submerged in water in a cup propped up against his schoolbag, the flowers that the little boy had picked were sinking like a forgotten promise. Rocked by the children's shouts echoing across the park, stretched out against each other, Bastien and his grandmother looked like they were sleeping.

Tiny stars.
Thousands of yellow stars.
I want to die.
Cousin, crush me in your arms
Make me die again.

7

The bed banged silently against the wall and the nightstand. The cushions that Martin had put behind the head of the metal bedframe were doing an admirable job. Only the woman persisted in making noise, alternating between plaintive groans and panting. To stifle her cries, Martin clamped a hand over her mouth, which only heightened their excitement. She bit him until she drew blood; he grew even more vigorous. Two glasses and a half-full whisky bottle clinked together on the nightstand as if toasting them, threatening to fall onto the rug. The woman's naked body disappeared under her massive, hairy partner. Lost within the crumpled sheets, an ankle slipped out, rubbing against the fabric to the rhythm of the battering. After a while, the man straightened up, lifting up his partner's legs and hooking them around his hips. He then penetrated her in a position that put the muscles in his arms and legs to the test. The woman had to find something other than his fist to bite.

When they'd caught their breath, uncovered to the waist and legs spread-eagled across the bed, a mobile rang. Martin had just fallen back to sleep. He barely opened his eyes and answered the call.

'Right, Martin. I can't stay here, really, knowing you're there all the time, even if you're doing it for my own good, that's it, it's just beyond me. Dr Mamnoue told me yesterday about an establishment in Hyères that would be very good for me. I'd be put up in an apartment with a balcony, a kitchenette for cooking and even a guest bed; I could have Bastien to stay over. It seems perfect to me. Did you come back late last night? I didn't hear you come in.'

'Good morning, Mum.'

'Yes, good morning, son. It's half eight, you know. Aren't you going to the surgery this morning?'

'Yes, yes, I'm going.'

The man sat on the edge of the bed and lit a cigarette.

'I thought that what you wanted most in life was getting back to your house and your garden,' he said, clearing his throat.

'You know full well that it isn't my house any more,

37

that it belongs to my son, and three years on, you've turned it into a slum.'

'Mum—'

'I can't stand being here any longer. I have to leave. Now that Bamboo and the cherry tree are dead, I couldn't care less about the garden. And you keep the furniture. I don't want to take anything with me. Why did you destroy the cage? You could have used it as a rabbit hutch—'

'Can we talk about this later?' Martin cut across her.

She began again, more sweetly: 'Ah. You're not alone, is that it? Who is it? Is it Audrette? Will I make you some coffee?'

Martin looked at the woman sprawled across his bed, who asked for a cigarette, two fingers to her parted lips. Her make-up had run, accentuating the wrinkles under her eyes. Her small breasts, rosy from lovemaking, gave her a youthful air, and the scar above her pubis told some of her story.

'Mum, I can't talk to you now. I'm going to hang up.'

'Dr Mamnoue said that the sun would do me a world of good, you know.'

'Yes, yes, he's right. We'll talk about it on my lunch break, OK?'

After throwing the phone in the middle of the sheets, Martin idly caressed his partner's chest.

'Who was that?' she asked.

'The landlady.'

'Pardon?'

'My mother. She thinks I'm with my ex-wife.'

The floorboards creaked. The woman stood and looked for her underwear in the jumble of laundry strewn about the floor and across the messy room. She was wearing the same sad expression that Martin had noticed the first time she had walked through the door of his surgery. He sat on the edge of the bed for a moment, studying his toes, scratching his cheeks through his beard. His neck was sore.

'Can I use your bathroom?'

The man grasped the bottle of whisky and poured himself a glass to swallow two tablets he had fished out of the nightstand.

'By all means, Valérie ... There are clean towels underneath the sink.'

Martin would see her again later for an appointment, like the others. And she wouldn't insist on their sleeping together again. Women don't like men who slip through life without looking for so much as a foothold.

Two floors down, a suitcase, flung against the stairs in the entryway, was still waiting to be unpacked. An old radio set was playing in the living room. Journalists were commenting on the news of the day: Vladimir Putin had officially taken up office as President of the Russian Federation, a contentious penalty shoot-out between

Nantes and Calais' amateur team in the finals of the Coupe de France, and the depraved behaviour of one Dr Martin Préau – a complete humiliation to his mother. Standing at the window, Mrs Préau drank her second cup of coffee, listening closely to water gurgling in the pipes. Someone was having a shower in her bathroom. Soap residue and the woman's hair were undoubtedly running through the plumbing in the house. Mrs Préau winced in disgust and spat her coffee into the sink.

SEEING WHAT
YOU WANT TO SEE

'I shall not go to war before having
tried all the arts and ways of peace.'

François Rabelais, *Gargantua*

8

The car's back wheel hit a pothole on the road. The bouquet of flowers bounced off the passenger's knees. Mrs Préau was shunted along the back seat closer to her son, wrapping an arm over his right shoulder.

The taxi driver was driving like a madman.

Both were agreed on this point.

The trip from the Gare de Lyon to Bagnolet seemed long. With the rain beating down, the car was now approaching a town in the eastern suburbs, marked out by shops with garish signs: takeaways, car accessory shops, estate agents, tool-hire places; Mrs Préau could barely recognise the city centre. After a dozen intersections, the taxi turned left into a driveway hedged with crape myrtle in full bloom. They passed a private secondary school where students in hoodies and young women in skinny jeans poured out for break time. Mrs Préau leaned her head against the glass, curious about this style – so unflattering for the heavy-set girls. The passenger finally recognised the railway bridge and the red bricks over which the car passed. Where a pretty forest of beech and chestnut had lined the road nine years earlier, a paltry square and two medical facilities (one retirement home and an assisted-living facility for the handicapped) had sprung up brazenly, along with a supermarket, topped off with a car park and surrounded by advertising hoardings. Directly opposite, a group of semi-detached houses was under construction. On the corner, an area of fifty square metres of grass clashed with a landscape dotted with bungalows; no doubt the planning handiwork of the town council, kept aside for the highest bidder.

'It's become so ugly,' exclaimed Mrs Préau.

A hand held onto her shoulder. Her son was trying to comfort her.

'We're almost there, Mum.'

A hundred metres to go. The road was restricted by a line of parked cars as it led towards the station.

'Take the next left and stop at the house with the green gates.'

Martin had taken the train with his mother early that morning. Mrs Préau had nothing more for baggage than a handbag and an old carpet bag. Most of her things had been moved the week before by a haulier from Hyères les Palmiers. A slightly sharp stop sent the bouquet of flowers sliding off the old woman's knees. Martin caught it before it could brush against her shoes. Nevertheless, neither Mrs Préau nor her son passed comment on the man's driving. They were eager to get out of the overheated vehicle, and to reach the end of their journey.

When she spotted the low wall that ran around the property, Mrs Préau felt her heart rate surge. Over time, the stones had blackened, eaten away by pollution. The pillars marking out the property line were missing a few pieces, giving their surfaces a grainy finish. Mrs Préau looked up to the chestnut tree, majestic behind the iron railings atop the wall. Out of the tortured frame of its trunk shot branches trimmed with buds. One sigh followed the next. With her helmet of grey hair in a bob, and her fine, pinched lips, Mrs Préau looked tiny beneath the umbrella her son held to protect her from the elements.

'You didn't get it cut down. Thank God for that.'

The bunch of keys jingled. Martin turned the handle of the front gate and pulled the suitcase across the paving stones in the garden up to the stone steps at the front door of the house. Mrs Préau stopped for a moment on the driveway, as if suspended from the umbrella, contemplating the desiccated shrubbery and flowerbeds that ran along the base of the house. She wondered how her son had managed to kill established plants that she had planted well before she left. Mrs Préau looked up, eyeing the roof. It hadn't suffered too much in the recent storms. The valleys below the slope of the roof were in good condition, and were casting rainwater away from the façade of the house, making up for the lack of gutters. Mrs Préau's vision became clouded; raindrops beaded on the surface of her glasses. She joined her son at the top of the steps.

9

What struck Mrs Préau was the smell. You never forget how a house smells. Hers smelled stale, of wax, and of shit. An explanation wasn't long in coming. With a hand-kerchief over his nose, Martin tried in vain to flush the toilets. One of the movers must have relieved himself before heading home for the night.

'Bastard. One of them shat in the toilet!'

He left his mother, crossed the hallway that was crowded with a dozen stacked boxes and headed for the stairs that led down into the basement. Mrs Préau guessed that her son meant to turn on the water and electricity mains. She folded her umbrella and leaned it against a cast-iron radiator to dry. The radiator was cold. Like the rest of the house. It would take several hours to get it warm again. Martin hadn't lived here in years. Mrs Préau didn't wait for her son to come back up from the basement, and took a few steps into the kitchen.

The place was strange to her. All of the furniture had been changed. It was the same in each room in the house. Louis XVI chests of drawers, art deco pedestal tables and plant stands, enamelware boxes, Regency mirrors and clocks, Louis-Philippe sideboards, porcelaine de Paris vases – their bourgeois family heirlooms left the house two years after Mrs Préau had moved to the south. At that time, her son had chosen to move closer to his surgery in Pavillons-sous-Bois, pronouncing the family home too vast for him. One Friday afternoon, men had come in a removals lorry and made a clean sweep of the place, ripping out everything down to the light fittings and the pink marble mantelpieces. All that was left was the upright piano on the first-floor landing, the piano on which Mrs Préau had learned to play herself, and then given musical theory lessons to a few students. It was daylight robbery. Mrs Préau's fine walnut dressing table now would belong to rich Americans who had paid too much for the antique. Some people stuff the sumptuous interior of their villas with authentic pieces like so much pocket change.

Mrs Préau put the flowers on the dining-room table and set about opening the shutters to air out the disgusting smell emanating from the bathroom. To her surprise, it was easy to fold back the metal shutters against the windowsills; this side of the house was less exposed to the elements. The variegated oleaster hedge had tripled in size and was turning yellow against the horizon, shielding the ground floor from the view of passers-by. A few red berries hung like baubles – little bayberries that tempted children, and that Bastien would put have put to his lips when he was little under his granny's anxious gaze.

Mrs Préau went into the living room to open the other shutters. Devoid of its leaves, the chestnut tree no longer hid the view.

Mrs Préau was horrified by what she discovered.

When she got out of the taxi, she had only been able to see the left side of the street, where her house was. There was nothing left of the immense woodland that stood opposite. Its owner had sold it off piecemeal, like the rest. A fox had once lived there, and the neighbourhood children would go there every summer to pilfer as many plums, cherries and gooseberries as they could hold in their bundled shirts. They would stick their scratched hands into the blackberry bushes, where a crucifix had been brightened up by a fountain from the turn of the last century. Two bungalows had appeared there, covered in outdated pebbledash. One was situated immediately in front of Mrs Préau's house, twenty or so metres away. A concrete wall, openwork at the top, marked out the plot.

Though a weeping birch partly hid the house, from the living room windows Mrs Préau could see part of the garage and a garden swing.

'They built them two years ago. A couple with children.'

Martin stood a few steps back from his mother. Trying to appear more relaxed, he spat into his handkerchief before putting it back in his pocket. 'When the chestnut is in leaf, it'll all be like it was before.'

Mrs Préau shook her head slowly.

No.

It will never be like it was before.

She said in a small voice, 'I feel like this is the first time I've ever been here, Martin.'

Mrs Préau raised a hand to caress her son's cheek. His skin was soft, soothing. She preferred Martin clean-shaven.

10

Mrs Préau received a visit from her son once a week, on Thursday. They regularly ate at Le Bistrot du Boucher in Villemomble. The menu hardly ever changed, which Mrs Préau rather liked. This evening they were celebrating her seventy-first birthday. She ordered the usual set menu: beef, green beans, wine and dessert. They brought her an *île flottante* covered in toasted almonds that was as heavy as a dictionary. Mrs Préau felt almost jubilant. It was a shame that Bastien wasn't there to distract her with his shenanigans, upending his juice across the tablecloth, pinching chips from his daddy's plate and sticking them up his nose.

As a matter of unshakeable habit, Mrs Préau would ask

her son a disagreeable question over dessert. She didn't miss her chance.

'Have you had any news from your father?'

Martin folded his napkin and pushed back his plate.

'No. But you could call him, you know.'

'I don't like the telephone, Martin. There's too much static on the line. I'm not sure that I even want to keep the phone in the house, for that matter. I think it's a needless expense.'

'I don't think so, Mum. You have to be able to reach me if there's a problem. And I want to be able to call you. You're not in an apartment building any more; you're alone in the house.'

'I was born in that house. What do you think could possibly happen to me?'

Mrs Préau grabbed her spoon. She furrowed her brow. Martin knew this expression well: the martyred mother.

'And besides,' she sighed, 'my son could easily come over from time to time for a chat instead of leaving me with some idiot nurse underfoot.'

'Mum, you know full well that we're understaffed – between being on call and being at the surgery, I'm over-whelmed with work.'

'It's lovely to write, too. It hones your spelling and grammar.'

'That's it, Mum. Get me some writing paper.'

'Oh no! I can't read a word of your chicken scratch. It's worse than your father's.'

Mrs Préau plunged her spoon into her dessert.

'I don't know how you did it, forgiving him for abandoning you,' she blurted as soon as she'd swallowed her first mouthful.

The man turned his napkin over to hide a stain.

'Mum, we're not going to talk about that again. It's you who told him to leave. Not the other way around.'

'Mmm. All the same, I was hardly in a position to feed my child and cover living expenses on my teacher's salary. Your father was well aware of that.'

Mrs Préau saw her son pull a familiar face. Her mouth was full of egg white and caramelised sugar, and Martin couldn't bear to listen to her speak with her mouth full. When he was a child, it would make him sick to his stomach. His parents' past troubles as a couple triggered a similar response; he had grown up with nausea. She knew how dearly Dr Martin Préau paid for dinner every Thursday with his mother – it was his cross to bear. He kept her company, stuck a fork into a piece of meat to put on a good show, but he didn't have the appetite for it. If he had indigestion once he got back to his apartment, Mrs Préau wouldn't have been the least bit surprised. She hurried to empty her mouth.

Martin leaned towards his mother's *île flottante*.

'All right, listen. I don't want to talk about Dad.

Besides, it's been thirty years. And you were already a headmistress.'

'Hmm. I'm not so sure about that. Still, do you remember how they "thanked" me when I was three years from retirement age?'

'You're confusing things. That was in 'ninety-seven. Be quiet and finish your dessert.'

'Fired for gross negligence – hah! It was slander, obviously. I didn't write a single letter to the County Council. That's not my style. They never had a thing on me.'

'You've already told me this a hundred times.'

'What's that in your pocket?'

Martin readjusted his jacket by the shoulders.

'It's nothing, Mum.'

'Because you're putting your hand in your inside jacket pocket a lot.'

'It's my wallet, that's all.'

'This *île flottante* is delicious.'

'Are you having a coffee?'

'No, thank you. It's your father who drinks coffee in the evening. Not me.'

Martin asked for the bill with the weariness particular to the children of divorced parents. He regretted feeling like he had to get a gift for his mother, again, and his choice was as obvious as a garden gnome in a flowerbed. He had unearthed on the Internet a little inlaid Louis XVI table in rosewood and sycamore with a pull-out writing desk. It was similar to the one that Mrs Préau had got from her great-grandmother, which had been stolen in the course of the famous burglary. It was an expensive present for Mrs Préau, who had refrained from sending anything to her son for his birthday for these last eight years, convinced that the package would be stolen by a postal worker before reaching its destination.

'Do you know that they don't need to open letters any more to read them? They use scanners, it's more practical. That's progress for you.'

Martin drove his mother back home without venturing a word. He was hiding something from her, something that he was ashamed of or that embarrassed him greatly. Something that probably had something to do with the fact that his mobile hadn't stopped vibrating in his inside jacket pocket throughout the meal.

He'd have to bring it up sooner or later.

It saddened Mrs Préau that her son could keep such secrets.

A close-knit family is built on honesty, not hushed-up problems.

11

The alarm clock rang at six forty-five. At seven thirty, Mrs Préau opened the shutters in her bedroom. Next, twenty minutes of morning gymnastics. Isabelle, the housekeeper, who lived around the corner, rang the doorbell at nine o'clock on the dot. She took off her shoes, stepped into her slippers, tied an apron around her hips and consistently refused the coffee offered to her by Mrs Préau. For an hour, Isabelle would dust or run the hoover, make the bed or take care of the laundry while the old woman would read in the living room, drinking a Nescafé. She belonged to the library and would take out two or three books per week. She took notes on each work, notes that she transcribed in large notebooks, to do with errors of style, implausibility or philosophical and historical details of interest to her, in addition to all biblical references. At eleven o'clock on Tuesdays and Thursdays, Mrs Préau had an appointment in the city centre with a physiotherapist, Mr Apeldoorn, to treat arthritis in her neck. Sessions in traction or with electro-stimulation meant that she could go without the foam brace that she was obliged to wrap around her neck while she gardened. On Wednesdays, after her nap, Mrs Préau would walk to Dr Mamnoue, in Raincy. On the way back, she would stop in the new square along the railway line and look for Bastien's face among the children. There, if time permitted, she would unwrap her snack (home-made biscuits or even an overly sweet pastry from Didier's in the Place du Général de Gaulle, accompanied by a flask of fruit juice), which she would eat on the bench, offering any crumbs from her little meal to the cheeky sparrows. On Fridays, Mrs Préau would devote the morning to writing a few letters, and the afternoon would be dedicated to the shopping. She would do her shopping at the supermarket, pulling her wheeled caddy behind her, buying nothing without having first consulted the ingredients of each product. Colourings, preservatives, thickening agents, sweeteners – she ruled out from her diet any product that could potentially cause cancer or cardiovascular disease. She selected her meat, fish, fruit and vegetables at the Saturday morning market, finding out about their country of origin, and always refusing tomatoes, oranges and strawberries from

Spain. Once a month, she would stock up at the health food shop on Avenue Jean Jaurès, where she would get herself some Indian soap nuts, margarine, dried fruit and evening primrose oil capsules. She only ate bread from the boulangerie-pâtisserie at Gagny station, where she had taken to going again. She inevitably chose a type of baguette called a *festive*, with a very well-baked, crunchy crust that was like biting into a firecracker on Bastille Day.

At seven, the same time that she had her dinner, Mrs Préau would prepare a tin bowl of food for the neighbourhood stray cats, which she would leave near the shed at the end of the garden. The shutters were closed at seven thirty. Mrs Préau had a light dinner in the dining room while watching the news on France 3, and then did some more reading before getting ready for bed. The bedside lamp was turned off at ten thirty. If she couldn't sleep, she'd count high-speed trains. The echo of their infernal race would reach her with reassuring regularity from the railway platform a hundred metres away.

On Saturdays, between nine and noon, a nurse, Ms Briche, would visit to check her blood pressure. If she picked up on the slightest agitation or sign of an anxiety attack in her patient, she informed Dr Martin Préau – which she had never had to do until now.

Sunday was the hardest day. On Sundays, Mrs Préau would fast, drinking vegetable soup and organic herbal teas concocted by Mrs Budin, the chemist. No one ever came to Mrs Préau on Sunday, and Mrs Préau had no one to visit. She didn't keep up any particular acquaintances among the neighbours, who kept to themselves. They were content to say hello as they passed each other on the footpath every other day when the bins went out. Only one of her former students, who lived in number four, sometimes stopped to smile or exchange pleasantries in front of Mrs Préau's house. Though she was in her fifties, Ms Blanche seemed twenty years older. The poor woman had lost her mind years ago. She filled her days by hoarding anything recyclable in her house, in her garden and even in the boot of her car. Cardboard boxes, bottles, corks, plastic wrappers, newspapers – fragile structures heaped like peaks of whipped cream were visible behind the outer fence where a tangle of shrubs clung, forming random snares. Having scaled the front wall, a clematis had meandered inside the house via the first-floor window that Ms Blanche left open throughout the year, and through which other piles of reusable materials were visible. The mind of the young woman who had once studied the piano at Mrs Préau's house had clearly meandered, too, and her clothes were impregnated by the smell of mould.

Sunday was a terrible day. The children weren't coming back from school, singing along the path; the postman wasn't doing his rounds, dinging his bicycle bell;

the ballet of dumper trucks and JCBs working on nearby building sites was brutally called to a halt; the windows of Mrs Préau's house weren't vibrating each time they passed; the street was deserted, the neighbourhood had been syphoned of all its commotion; not even a one-eyed tomcat snuck across the dew-covered garden.

So Mrs Préau would watch the neighbours.

12

High-pitched screams and the squeak of a swing forced Mrs Préau out of her Sunday nap at about three o'clock. She got up, opened the double curtains and discovered the children playing in the garden. A little girl and two boys. The smaller of the two boys was barely more than three and was snivelling a lot, the victim of his sister's taunts. Aged five or six perhaps, she was deliberately making him fall out of the swing, grabbing the ball from his hands or pushing him off a little truck so that she could take his place. She was using her physical superiority with some skill, taking advantage of the lack of supervision by either her mother or her father. For their part, they were happy enough to glance over at their children when they got too rowdy. Occasionally, the father came out to smoke a cigarette and drink a coffee or a beer. He would sit on a plastic garden chair, and would pay the most attention to his mobile phone. The mother rarely appeared outside the house; she would charge across the garden, but only to take down the laundry that was hanging in front of the wall of the garage. Both were blond of a rather Nordic sort, like the little boy and his sister.

The other boy, the bigger one, had dark, chestnut-brown hair. He must have been Bastien's age, seven or perhaps eight years old. He stood apart from the other two. He stayed in his corner beneath the weeping birch, calmly collecting stones and pieces of twigs so that he could arrange them on the paving stones in the garden. Invisible from the street, hidden by the cypress trees and the concrete wall, he no doubt thought that he was protected. Other than Mrs Préau's tall, fieldstone house, none of the nearby houses were high enough to over-look that part of the garden. Sitting at the little inlaid table that she had placed in a corner of the room near the window, the old woman would witness the children's games, nostalgic for the games that she used to oversee at break time when she was still teaching at the Blaise Pascal School. Soothed by the familiar hubbub that reigned in her neighbours' garden, she would occupy her hands by mending or sorting through everything she could in the house: buttons, ribbons, nuts and bolts, pencils, bills, family photographs, letters, postcards or drawings by former students. Sometimes, when the girl went too far, torturing her little brother for the fun of it, Mrs Préau would lean against the lace half-curtain. She adjusted her glasses and bit her lip. Certainly it would have been nice to play the role of the schoolmistress again, to open the window and give the little girl a stern warning. Best not get involved. Mrs Préau allowed herself the right to go to speak to the parents only if the little girl crossed the line. As for the child underneath the tree, he was of such exemplary intelligence that he would get curious. One Sunday after the next, he would go through the same motions, constructing totems with bundled twigs and flat stones. He was still, whether crouched or standing, gazing out into the curtain of cedars. No doubt he was looking at insects. And then, sometimes, he would look up suddenly in the direction of Mrs Préau's house. She would jerk back, dropping her box of buttons or the pile of photos propped on the writing drawer. With her fringe mussed, she'd pick up the things she had dropped, blushing. Wasn't it a sin to covet the fruits of your neighbour's garden?

It became a habit. Every Sunday and school holiday. As soon as Mrs Préau heard the strident shouts of the little boy and his sister's laugh, wherever she was at that moment, weeding the rockery, picking plums or figs from the branches, making jam with the fruit from the garden, writing a letter to her son or copying out a whole chapter from the memoir of a sergeant-major who once served under Napoleon, she would go straight back to her lookout post.

24 July 2009

Dear Martin,

You kindly offered to come and help me pick the many plums in the garden before you head off on holiday, but it's not necessary, as I'm working away at it each morning when it's cool. And they've almost all fallen. The ones still on the branch are rotten. Same with the fig tree. This hasn't been a good year for fruit. They were in bud too early in the season. They would have suffered from the frost.

On Sunday on the phone, I thought you seemed worried about me. The fact of being alone has never been a problem, you know. I've been living this way for twenty-eight years and it doesn't bother me at all any more. I saw Isabelle this morning and gave her two kilos of plums as well as some sheets that I wanted to get rid of. The ones from your room. As long as they're of use for something. She's leaving for Portugal at the end of July and will be back at the beginning of

September. Not worth replacing her, I'll get along
perfectly well without her – the house hardly gets dirty
if you don't leave the windows open during the day
(Oh, the dust from that bothersome building site at the
top of the road is collecting everywhere thanks to their
trucks full of rubble!) and I'm hardly overwhelmed by
laundry. Mr Apeldoorn, the physio, is also on holiday.
But Dr Mamnoue is taking appointments until mid-
August.

I find the neighbourhood changed. The people who
take the RER in the morning to go to work park their
cars any which way in the street. It's not unusual for
the young ones to gather next to the old wall of the
house, smoking and drinking beer. Nothing too bad,
but I'd prefer they do it elsewhere all the same.
Particularly when they turn up the volume on their
radios.

The heat has been getting to me a bit. These last few
days have been particularly hot and I haven't left the
house. The temperature is bearable, as I keep the shutters
closed. I'm really going to need something to help me
sleep, as I'm sleeping rather badly with the heat. No
more than five hours per night. Could you write me up
a prescription before you leave for Corsica? Bastien will
no doubt enjoy the holidays alone with his daddy. I
dream of spending a few days down there. Perhaps I
will.

I'd be very happy if my little grandson thought to send me a postcard this year.

Love and kisses,

Mum

13

Mrs Préau benefitted from very good eyesight for her age. Nonetheless, it was difficult for her to see beyond a certain distance, even with her glasses. So, she decided at the beginning of August to get some opera glasses from her optician, Mr Papy.

The reason was the little boy under the weeping birch. The lack of contact between him and the rest of the family intrigued her. It no doubt stemmed from a solitary temperament and a tendency on his part to be withdrawn. Yet his unwillingness to speak to the point of submission was unique. He never held a toy in his hands; he was content with twigs and stones. And though Mrs Préau did pass the younger brother and sister from time to time on the path as they were coming home from the bakery with their father, one on their bike, the other on a scooter, not once had the old woman ever seen the little boy behind them. And that was troubling.

It was a rainy Sunday when Mrs Préau first took her opera glasses out of their box. Taking advantage of a break in the weather, the children had come out to play in the garden, avoiding the puddles of water that had formed here and there on the lawn. The glasses allowed her to confirm her suspicions. The magnification showed up plenty of detail. Details had always ruled Mrs Préau's life. That's what made her so formidable when it came to marking school books.

As the weeks passed, the old woman noted in a black moleskin notebook the behaviour and attitudes of the child. She remarked, for example, that the little boy did not go out in the garden other than on the Lord's Day, not even during school holidays. The clothes that he wore were dirty, and seemed to be the same: trousers that were too short or shorts, a red sweatshirt or yellow T-shirt, trainers or flip-flops. His wrists were skinny, his skin greyish and he often scratched his head. The child probably suffered from vitamin deficiencies. His hygiene was dubious, too, which was not the case for either his sister or his younger brother.

Mrs Préau noted another important detail in her notebook to do with the little boy's behaviour. When he appeared on the porch, he never went out to play. He

71

would rub his eyes as if he were dazzled, and then come down the few stairs with unsteady steps.

But what bothered Mrs Préau more than anything was the resemblance to Bastien. The boys weren't just the same age. Both had pale eyes and curly chestnut hair, thin, short lips and an oval face.

From this point on, Mrs Préau couldn't think of her grandson without imagining the 'stone boy', as she called him in her notebook. She liked both boys in their own way.

14

Dr Mamnoue was the first person Mrs Préau spoke to about her neighbours. She did so prudently, without revealing too much, with the same care that she took putting on her make-up to go to his office.

'The child who doesn't play with the others is bothering you?'

'I wouldn't go that far. Let's say that I'm wondering about him.' Mrs Préau answered in her soft and somewhat broken voice. Dr Mamnoue hardly spoke louder than she.

'He is no doubt looking for some peace and quiet.'

'Yes, no doubt. But it's never a good sign, which I say from experience. A child who doesn't play with others in the playground is a child with problems, half the time.'

Mrs Préau often made reference to her experience as a teacher in her discussions with Dr Mamnoue. They covered fascinating subjects to do with the education and psychology of children. During her working life, Mrs Préau had had to come face to face with a few cases of maltreatment: there was one little girl, for example, who, after having been no doubt loved and wanted, grew up in an environment that was hugely psychologically violent. Isolated and criticised by her brothers and sisters who refused to play with her, the little girl suffered from bed-wetting until she was ten years old. Exhausted, her mother eventually stopped washing the sheets, making do with just drying them on the line. She was hit by her father for her poor marks, even though she was clearly unable to concentrate in class. The child was so afraid of her mother that when Mrs Préau called them both into the headmistress's office, the little girl fainted.

'So you think that by simply observing a person, you can find out everything about their life?' asked Dr Mamnoue.

'No. These are only warning signs. Then you have to confirm them.'

The man, who was slightly older than his patient, interlaced his fingers across his stomach and tipped his neck back in his leather armchair. A flyaway strand of hair fell coquettishly across the crown of his head.

'And am I to suppose, dear Elsa, that's what you intend to do?'

Mrs Préau smiled. She liked it when he called her by her first name, just as she liked that he felt the same way. They had begun this ritual many years ago, well before she treated herself to a relaxing break at Hyères les Palmiers.

'I have no idea at the moment, Claude. We'll see. First I have to get rid of all that dust.'

'Yes, it's incredible.'

Dr Mamnoue picked back up the glass jar filled with ochre dust and gravel. He weighed it in his hand.

'You wouldn't think that trucks would leave behind so much dirt.'

'That is three months' worth, though it has eased up a bit since the beginning of August. They're a sight to be seen, driving down the road like madmen. Sometimes you can hear the gravel bouncing all the way up to the windows. The whole house shakes from it. Worse than the night freight train that passes at two forty-five.'

'Two forty-five?'

'Except Sundays and holidays.'

Mrs Préau produced the little moleskin notebook from her handbag to prove her point. She had the look of a schoolgirl who knew her recitation off by heart. Dr

Mamnoue nodded his head, then returned the jar to his desk, making the pebbles tinkle against its surface. The wrinkles across his brow were like furrows waiting for planting.

'That reminds me of when I was a little boy. I had an incredible collection of stones that I put in a jar just like this. Didn't you?'

Mrs Préau responded cheekily that the only thing she had collected didn't fit in a jar.

'Oh really? So what did you collect?'

'Poltergeists. Or hairbrushes belonging to my class-mates at boarding school. Whichever took my fancy.'

15 August 2009

Dear Mr Mayor,

Allow me to direct your attention to the troubles that the residents of Rue des Lilas, among whom I number, have been enduring of late. Our road, which is close to the town train station, is not supposed to be used for parking by RER users. Yet this is now the case, and every two weeks, we are reminded of this fact by a concerto of car horns. As you know, the parking is on one side of the road only, and twice each month, cars must park along the path on the opposite side. As you might imagine, the residents respect this rule, which is not the case for the drivers who park on our street without paying the slightest bit of attention to any of the signs before leaving to take their trains. The result is that they disrupt the traffic very severely, even going so far as to block any cars from passing at all.

You understand, Mr Mayor, that this situation is trying for the residents. I know better than to suggest to you that parking on alternate sides of the road on Rue des Lilas be revoked, as it is already challenge enough with the noise pollution and the damage to property walls and the gates to our houses caused by RER users on Saturday nights and the nights before Bank Holidays. Our letterboxes were 'repainted' at the beginning of August, and the path laid with broken glass from beer bottles.

Personally, I have twice found empty cans and other detritus (an empty cigarette packet, a chocolate bar wrapper) in my garden, which had been thrown over the fence.

It would be wise to consider increasing surveillance on some of those streets more prone to passing vandalism than others. It would be a shame for our lovely properties – which are the heart and soul of this town – to have to be decked out in barbed wire and watchtowers to guarantee their occupants a bit of peace.

I am sure that you will handle this matter with the due diligence that it deserves.

Respectfully yours,

Mrs Elsa Préau
Born, raised and living locally for more than fifty years

15

An apple waited for breakfast time in a ramekin on the little table. With a gilet over her shoulders, Mrs Préau was putting drawings from the oldest children in her junior school classes – 1975–1981 – in alphabetical order. The attic was stuffed with boxes full of the archives of her old school. Mrs Préau took great satisfaction in looking back over the drawings in which the parents are often depicted as grotesque, covered in hair, or as matchstick men. The princesses drawn by little girls born in the 1960s were adorned with multicoloured beads and princess tent dresses with balloon sleeves. As for the knights who appeared under the boys' paintbrushes, they were bent under the weight of their fabulous swords, fighting at the gates of fortified castles or felling their jagged walls. Pokey cars threatened to fall into ravines, and they never forgot the aerial on the roof of the house or the smoke coming out of the chimney. Then the children began drawing satellite dishes on balconies and square fish on plates.

Mrs Préau glanced at the neighbours' garden where under a grey sky the little brother and sister were ripping each other to shreds to see who would get the Frisbee. Motionless as ever, the stone boy remained under the weeping birch, playing by bouncing gravel in his hands. Several times he scratched a scab on his right elbow, and made the wound bleed, before throwing his stones again. Mrs Préau abandoned her sorting for a moment to write down in her notebook: *Child's self-destructive behaviour. Signs of scarring.* Then the phone rang in the living room and she had to leave her lookout post to go down and answer it.

'Mum, it's Martin.'

'Ah. Right. How are you, son? Are your holidays going well? It's already autumn here.'

The conversation lasted for twenty minutes: Martin reluctantly explained why his mother would have to make do with monthly dinners with him once he returned from Corsica.

'You've had enough of me then, is that it? You'd rather bed your patients than eat a plate of chips with your mother?'

'Mum, you're spiteful, I'm hanging up.'

'I'm not an idiot, you know.'

'You don't know anything. You know nothing about my life, Mum. You never did.'

'Oh, but I do!'

Finally, he decided to let the cat out of the bag.

'I'm back with Audrette. We've got back together.'

Mrs Préau pulled up a chair to the side table where the phone sat. She was not quite sure she could continue standing. The return of her ex-daughter-in-law to her son's life was the worst news she could have heard.

'How long have you been hiding the truth from me?' she said flatly.

'A year.'

'And that's why we can't have dinner together on Thursdays any more?'

'Yes.'

'She doesn't want you to see your mother?'

'Now, that's not really it. Audrette thinks that—'

'You do what you like, Martin. It's all the same to me. As soon as I've heard from my grandson ... A propos, how is Bastien? He still hasn't sent me a postcard.'

When Mrs Préau had finished her conversation and returned to her room, the neighbours' garden had been emptied of its occupants, which greatly upset her.

Mrs Préau left the bread in the toaster for too long. She dined on onion soup with an aftertaste of sulphur, listening to the newsreader on France 3 summarise the cases of swine flu in France. At nine, a fight broke out among the tomcats in the garden near the shed. Mrs Préau had to go out in her slippers and dressing gown to restore order and chase away the one-eyed cat who liked to wreak havoc. Then she closed and bolted the door. She turned off her bedside lamp as usual at half ten.

At ten past midnight, Mrs Préau switched on the bedside lamp, awoken with a start by a noise coming from inside the house, on the floor below. The sound of metal being struck violently, followed by a muffled cry and an animal's moan. She listened, motionless under the covers, her heart beating.

It will not start again. It must not start again.

Mrs Préau thought things through. She had put the heating back on that morning. The woodwork was settling, creaking out its displeasure. The metal shutters were warped, victims of the wintry night. And the cats were tearing strips off of each other in the garden, which was disputed territory. But the most rational explanation did not cure her fear. A moment later, she was walking around the house, hammer in hand, turning on the lights one by one. Going around the house with a tool that belonged to her father, she inspected every room, every nook, looking behind the doors, and then swallowed one of the pills prescribed by her son to clear up any nightmares – ah, that was better.

At twelve forty-five, the hammer went back into the drawer of the bedside table. Mrs Préau noted the time the noise had occurred in her notebook, and then lay down again, leaving the hall light on, like when she was a little girl and her mother came to see her as a surprise.

16

The area around the train station was just a vast construction site. The roar of dumper trucks spewing their contents of earth and rubble on land sold off by the municipality for the construction of a private residence and a rehabilitation centre joined the dogs barking at the noise of the pneumatic drills that hurt their ears.

Isabelle ran the brush along the kitchen windowsill outside with a sigh. More ochre dust!

'When will they finish the construction work?'

A few metres away, Mrs Préau was cutting back the plants in the rockery for the winter, her neck wrapped in the foam brace.

'We're lucky, Isabelle. Imagine the hell that the people

on Rue des Petits Rentiers are living, with that huge crane overhead and a cement mixer that lets its motor run all day. That smell of diesel is horrific.'

The housekeeper nodded with a sad smile, holding her dustpan across her body.

'Will I put all this in the jar as usual?'

'Do, Isabelle. Do.'

She returned to the kitchen, saying to Mrs Préau that they were almost out of floor cleaner and Ajax for the windows, but that there was no hurry. The housekeeper felt the ground vibrate under her slippers. A truck was going down the road, giving the barking dogs a second wind. Mrs Préau also felt the vibration but paid no attention, too busy using the handle of the shears to crush a family of spiders nestled in the rockery.

'Mrs Elsa?'

The housekeeper stuck her head out the living-room window. She sounded concerned, like she was doubting herself.

'Yes, Isabelle?'

'Could you come and look, please?'

Mrs Préau straightened up, attached the shears to the belt of her overalls and went back to the steps. She tapped the heels of her rubber boots against the scraper fixed to the wall, and as nothing was stuck to the soles, she went inside. Isabelle was still leaning out of the living-room window, staring at the stone windowsill.

'What did you find?'

'The stones. It's strange.'

Isabelle rolled the gravel a few centimetres with her brush. A stain appeared on a stone. Mrs Préau raised her eyebrows.

'Looks like dried blood.'

The gravel was also covered in the same red colour. Isabelle shook her head, muttering.

'That's all we need!'

Taken aback, Mrs Préau stood still for a moment.

'What should I do, Mrs Elsa? Should I put them in the jar, too?'

Mrs Préau took off her neck brace with an irritated gesture.

'Leave it. I'll take care of it.'

She waited until the housekeeper had gone home before she spread the small stones across the kitchen table and looked at them under a magnifying glass, turning them over carefully in her hands. It was not a trick. They were stained with dried blood. How had these stones landed on the living-room windowsill? Where could the blood possibly have come from? The stones slid into a jam jar. Mrs Préau screwed the lid on tightly, and then looked for a place to store the jar. She decided that the best hiding place was the crisper drawer of the refrigerator. Back in the living room, Mrs Préau stood in front of the window: the neighbours' weeping birch was ten metres across the street, the exact location where the child usually stood. Mrs Préau put a hand over her mouth, thinking. Was it possible that the child had thrown the stones? That the blood had come from the cut on his elbow? Up until now she had attributed the presence of small stones and gravel on the windowsills to passing trucks. Could there be another explanation? Had the boy already thrown stones into her garden? By not aiming too high, somehow, you could reach the living-room window without the chestnut leaves getting in the way.

The tree's mottled foliage trembled in the breeze. A strand of grey hair tickled Mrs Préau's nose. She brushed it away, pulling the little black notebook out of the pocket of her overalls and jotting down the date and time at which the stones had been discovered. She also wrote two questions:

Why would the child have thrown the blood-covered stones against my window?

Is there a connection to the noise heard in the middle of the night last night?

She went to her room to find a pair of binoculars to take a look in the neighbours' garden. It was empty. There didn't seem to be any movement in the house. Only the barking of dogs in the street repeated like an echo distorted by the wind. Mrs Préau sat on her bed. It was a Monday. It was almost noon. She would have to wait until Sunday to see the child behind the concrete wall. She had a week to think about what to believe.

17

It rained for six days. Mrs Préau only went out to go to medical appointments, neglecting her shopping and returning her books to the library. She made do with meals based on tinned food accompanied by thawed frozen bread. Wednesday's session with Dr Mamnoue was devoted to the reappearance of her ex-daughter-in-law in Martin's life. She associated unpleasant memories with Audrette and was relieved to offload the more cumbersome ones. On Thursday, Martin had to cancel their dinner; in the four days since he returned from Corsica, the waiting room at his office hadn't once emptied before half eight. He was skipping meals, abusing vitamin bars and caffeinated fizzy drinks. A real Samaritan. He was working his way to a lovely ulcer. Just like his father used to do. Foolish.

On Sunday, no one appeared in the neighbours' soggy garden. The shutters remained closed throughout the day. Mrs Préau didn't see the car come out of the garage. Perhaps the family had gone away? When Mrs Préau telephoned her son at the end of the day, he refused to put Bastien on the line. At half past seven, she ate a vegetable soup in front of the France 3 national news. The news was pathetic: the threat of a flu epidemic was growing, the release of a video of Brice Hortefeux's polemical comments was raising an outcry on the left, a collection of school supplies was now being organised for the poorest families, a report showed the dilapidated and insalubrious state of university dormitories, a British artist had found nothing better to do than to put a mould of his head covered with his own blood on show in London. But the regressive aspect of society today designed to shun the values of the Republic was not the source of Mrs Préau's annoyance. She knew that mankind was condemned to die of cancer, poisoned by antibiotics, volatile chemical compounds in paints, preservatives and parabens in cosmetics, its belly full of its own waste plastic, like an albatross at Midway Atoll in the North Pacific, and she did not care.

No, what was worrying her was the big, one-eyed tomcat.

Mrs Préau's garden was a haven for stray animals. No conflict was tolerated. The one-eyed cat had made up his mind to prevent his fellow strays access to the food dishes left near the garden shed. He didn't care about getting scraped and collecting scars, flaunting them with all the childish arrogance of a dominant male. Recently, an abscess on his left front leg had burst. Blood and pus were seeping from it, dirtying the food dishes. Mrs Préau could not approach him to take care of it – he was a really aggressive cat, and the wound only made him worse. So she chased him away when she saw him jump over the garden wall, knowing that at night, when she wasn't there, he would return to do his worst and win back any territory he decided belonged to him.

Mrs Préau had always taken care of the animals around her. Once an active member of and volunteer for the Society for the Protection of Animals, she had gone so far as to collect a goat with two broken legs found at a motorway rest stop on the way to Provins and a young baboon rescued from a cosmetics laboratory that had been paying a whopping amount of business tax to the Champagne-Ardenne regional government. But if a despot terrorised and deprived others of their food, even if he was one-eyed and mangy, that was too much to bear.

She had to do something.

At eight o'clock, Mrs Préau was ready. Positioned in the shed on a stool, hidden under a plastic tarp, she waited until the cat showed the tip of his nose at the jam-packed bowls, shaking a box of cat food to attract him.

'Come on, come here, you.'

It took a good quarter of an hour before the lame cat dared to enter the dark shack, inhaling the cat food piece by piece that trailed to the stool where his benefactor stood.

'Come on, my fat tomcat, come here.'

Mrs Préau's voice was soft and quavering. He was so close to her that she could feel him purring.

'I think it's about time the feast came to an end, young man.'

The shock of the hammer against the cat's skull cut the soft purring short.

15 September 2009

Ms Blanche,

There is currently a rumour in the neighbourhood that you engage in strange practices in your ramshackle house. From my bedroom window, I saw you last night, by the light of a pink moon, rocking a cradle in which, according to local residents (so says the butcher), is the body of a dead dog.

I should tell you that I am not one of those people who point the finger at others as in times gone by. I do not believe in the modern-day witches the tabloids buy into. I think that if you didn't forget to wash, and if you cleared out a bit of your clutter, they wouldn't talk so much rubbish about you. In the eyes of our neighbours, you would simply be a poor woman who cannot bring herself to bury her pet, powerless to tame the melancholy of her heart.

If I can help in any way, please let me know; I just buried a cat in my garden, and I'm only a few shovelfuls of earth away.

With fond memories of the music lessons that I gave you, Delphine, a happy time in a past life,

In solidarity,

Elsa Préau

18

Dr Mamnoue was quite fond of the dreams of his oldest patient. She had a talent as a storyteller that gave credibility and gravitas to her tales. The previous night, a nightmare had woken her well before dawn. She immediately noted its contents in her notebook, which was now open on her lap.

'It was night-time. There was someone in the house. A presence more disturbing than hostile. And that someone was playing the piano downstairs in the living room. The melody wasn't anything familiar, and I didn't know if the tune was happy or sad. I was terrified to leave my bed, and my bedside lamp refused to turn on. Then I got up to turn on the overhead light, but the switch didn't work either. The electricity had been cut off in the house.'

'Were you afraid?'

'I knew I had no choice but to go down to the cellar to flip the circuit breaker, and yes, I was very afraid to confront the person playing the piano. But I needed to know who was hiding in there. So I decided to feel my way down the stairs. When I reached the room, I saw the window that looks out onto the street fighting the wind and the curtains shaking as if they were angry.'

'The window was *fighting*, and the curtains were *angry*?' queried Dr Mamnoue.

Mrs Préau sighed, annoyed.

'Not exactly. Let's say they danced. They moved erratically, fitfully. You see?'

'Continue, Elsa.'

'At the end of the room, sitting at the piano, was a young boy. I went to him to ask him what he was doing sitting in the dark. Then he turned to me. His face was covered with dirt. He said: "Play for me, Granny Elsa." Dirt also came out of his mouth. It was scary.'

Mrs Préau was quiet. She closed the notebook and crossed her hands over her knees. The old man cleared his throat.

'The child, was he Bastien?'

'It was ... yes. Yes, it was definitely Bastien.'

'And that was all?'

'That was all.'

'So ... '

'So . . . what?'

'I suppose that you've analysed your dream.'

Mrs Préau nodded. Her mouth was dry. She took the empty glass in front of her on the desk.

'I'd like a bit more water, please, Claude,' she said in a hoarse voice.

The doctor took the carafe behind him on a sideboard and filled his patient's glass.

'Well, what is your interpretation?'

The old woman drank the glass down in large gulps. Then she put it back on the desk with another sigh.

'I'm worried about the little boy who lives across the street.'

Then she added, almost ashamed: 'And I think I very much want to get back to the piano.'

The doctor tutted.

'Do you dream of Bastien often?'

'Almost never.'

'That's what I thought.'

'In fact, since I've started taking the pills Martin prescribed for me, I don't have dreams any more.'

'And you miss Bastien.'

'Yes.'

Dr Mamnoue shook his head.

'You find that hard to accept.'

'Accept what? That I miss Bastien?'

He tugged lightly on the collar of the shirt sticking

out from under his green cardigan and changed the subject.

'Do you feel at ease in your home?'

'It's my childhood home.'

'It's full of memories. Perhaps too many, right?'

Mrs Préau shrugged. With her long skirt and purple polo neck, she looked like a Little Sister of the Poor.

'Memories are part of life. I don't see how that can be disturbing.'

Dr Mamnoue joined his fingers together under his chin and put his elbows on his desk.

'And the earth in Bastien's mouth? How do you interpret that?'

A fire engine went down the road. Mrs Préau started when she heard the siren.

'Oh! Yes. Where is my head? That's just it! I forgot to tell you about it.'

'What?'

'I've had trouble with the cats.'

'Cats?'

'The neighbourhood stray cats. I feed them from time to time. One of them – he's very aggressive – attacks the others, but that's all over now.'

'What happened?'

Mrs Préau whispered maliciously.

'He's eating dirt.'

There was no more mention of Mrs Préau's dream for

the rest of the session. Dr Mamnoue took the fee for the session, shook his patient's hand and accompanied her to the landing outside.

'And don't forget, at night before you go to sleep: camomile tea with honey, and you'll sleep better.'

'If Martin could hear you, he'd laugh out loud. Natural medicines aren't his cup of tea.'

'I have nothing against chemicals, but let's try not to abuse them too much for the moment. I'd prefer that we see each other twice per week than give you sleeping tablets.'

'Two times per week? I didn't think you were so extravagant, Claude.'

The old man gave a faint smile.

'Right. We'll talk about it again next Wednesday. Goodbye, Elsa.'

Once outside, Mrs Préau hurried by the window of the patisserie on Place du Raincy. She didn't go in to buy cake, eager to escape her slip of the tongue, her only lie: it wasn't Bastien's face that she had seen in her dream, it was the stone boy's.

Play for me, Granny Elsa.

She couldn't wait for Sunday.

There was plenty to do between now and then.

19

The bell rang briefly. A moment later, students burst out of the school like bees from a hive, eager to get rid of their schoolbags. At the gate, some parents caught their offspring mid-flight with warm kisses. Among them, Mrs Préau's neighbour scanned the crowd for her children. A few metres behind on the opposite pavement, the former headmistress of the school observed the half-four pick-up time, hands in the pockets of her plum wool coat. The sky was blue, the air chilly, and most of the children wore scarves. It was one of the first days of autumn that heralded the winter, bright and proud.

It didn't take long for Mrs Préau to see the little boy, trailing his scarf on the ground, and then his sister, walking briskly towards their mother. She took her children by the hand and headed back towards their home without dawdling. She didn't speak to any other mums, and did not stop at the junior school, the main building of which backed onto the infant school, to wait for her eldest son. Mrs Préau was only partially surprised. It seemed logical. In cases of abuse, the child doesn't receive the same treatment as his brothers and sisters. The little boy no doubt went home alone. After all, at seven, you're a big boy, right? Mrs Préau remained sceptical: she had never seen the stone boy walking down the street. And there was only one entrance to his house, the gate facing her home. Unless the father went to fetch his son in the car after supervised study? Possibly. The old woman shook her head and returned to her place at the school gates, unable to resist the pleasure of watching school pick-up time.

All students in the school who weren't staying on for after-school activities streamed past, bringing back memories. Mrs Préau thought she saw Bastien at the age of three, on his first day of school, passing by wearing new brown calfskin lace-ups. A little one with his arm in a sling reminded her of Bastien aged five, when he hurt himself falling off his bike. In the midst of all the happy meetings, a little girl was screaming for no reason, firmly carried off by her rather ashamed father. The parents didn't linger as long as they did when she still ran the place: they were in a hurry to get back, and wrapped up short conversations, heading straight to Monoprix with the buggy. Modern family living favoured isolation and withdrawal. The lack of communication between individuals insured the State against any mobilisation, and eradicated any breeding grounds for social activism. Society was working steadily towards mental manipulation and marginalisation.

The flow of students dried up.

Mrs Préau sighed.

There were two hypotheses she could consider: the boy stayed on to study until six o'clock and she would have to wait until then, or he was at home, suffering. She would have to make enquires at the school. But under what pretext could she make such a move? She didn't even know the child's surname: her neighbours' postbox was marked only with the initials 'PD'.

'Are you waiting for a student?'

Mrs Préau started. On the other side of the fence at the Blaise Pascal Junior School, a beautiful woman in her forties was staring at her.

'Are you little Damien Delcroix's grandmother, madam?'

This was presumably the headmistress of the school.

'He was ill this morning, his dad picked him up at two this afternoon. Did he not tell you?'

Mrs Préau smiled at her sweetly. It was time to reveal her identity.

20

Open, sesame!

Being in the school where she had been the head-mistress for many years brought it all back to Mrs Préau. Other than a coat of paint and new floors, little had changed. The school had been entirely renovated, but the shape and size of the classrooms, the windows, the location of the toilets, the canteen and kitchens that they shared with the infant school, everything was there, exactly the same, even her small office to the left of the entrance to the playground.

'This will be a flying visit – I haven't much time.'

The headmistress, Mrs Mesnil, went ahead of her, trotting along in a belted black dress, showing her around her establishment with a degree of self-importance. A long pearl necklace rubbed against her mohair vest. There wasn't a single crease in her black Lycra tights where they met her polished ankle boots. She was new to the area and had taken over the school just that year. Its syllabus for the children was full of outings and various artistic activities. Their 'Flavour of the Day', for example, was a daily morning snack designed to promote trying new foods. The brand-new headmistress made it a point of pride to adhere to national guidelines.

'The school aims to make the students independent in their learning and responsible for it, but we strive for each child to succeed.'

The headmistress swept her fringe back into place. Providing access to culture writ large was also a priority for all students, 'whatever their standard of living'.

Mrs Préau liked the idea. But it was nothing new to her; it was the very foundation of her teaching for years before she was gently pushed towards the door.

'In addition, we are fortunate here to have a great educational tool at our disposal in our Nature and Garden class, where students learn to plant and maintain plants to discover and respect nature.' Mrs Préau asked her host if she knew who had the idea to create this Nature and Garden workshop in 1991. The headmistress raised her eyebrows, impressed.

'No – you? That's great! Did you know that Blaise Pascal became a pilot school because of it?'

Seeing that she had now made it into her good books, Mrs Préau asked if it were possible for her to see one or two classrooms. To her glee, the headmistress agreed.

Bright, decorated with drawings, with its little kitchenette and ironing corner, paint pots, box of cuddly toys and pretty books to read, the reception classroom made you want to curl up in it.

'Here is my class.'

Above the desk, a photo showed the children gathered in front of the blackboard. Mrs Préau immediately approached and put on her glasses. Sitting cross-legged to the left of the teacher, she recognised the little one who was his sister's whipping boy. Chance had smiled.

She pointed to the child in the photograph.

'Oh! I know this little face.'

'Kévin Desmoulins? His big sister is with Mr Di Pesa, with the older children.'

Mrs Préau was delighted. She hadn't managed to hear the name of the child screamed by his sister in the garden. The little girl, however, was frequently told off by her parents.

'Little Laurie, no?' she said, with feigned affection.

'Yes. Laurie is a good enough student. Kévin is more average. He finds it hard to concentrate. But they both seem to keep up.'

'And the elder brother? Is he also at Blaise Pascal?'

The headmistress raised her eyebrows, dubious. 'The

elder brother? There are only two Desmoulins children, to my knowledge.'

'Are you sure?'

'I can check their registration file but I think so.'

Mrs Préau felt her heart rate rise. She removed her glasses clumsily. A cowlick appeared in her fringe. The headmistress glanced at her watch.

'Would you like to see Laurie's class? I have five more minutes.'

The old lady stammered a reply. 'I wouldn't want to be a bother; I know how exhausting a school day can be for a teacher and a headmistress ...'

'You're not wrong there! But I can certainly give you a few minutes. It must be emotional for you, no?'

'Pardon?'

'To come back here, to your school.'

'Yes, very moving.'

'It's this way; we have to take the stairs.'

Mr Di Pesa's classroom was less fun but equally cheering and covered with photos. An alphabet of letters corresponding to animals ran around the walls. Boards on learning to count with fruits and vegetables were pinned above the blackboard. One entire wall was studded with drawings.

'Earlier this year,' the headmistress explained, 'this teacher asked his students to draw their families. Each child drew their house, their parents and siblings. It's a good exercise. It allows us to place the child in relation to their perception of things and make a preliminary assessment of their capabilities. Some are still struggling to hold a pencil . . . '

Mrs Préau took off her glasses. She could see the amazing works of young artists: scrawny dads, chubby mums, giant dogs on leads, houses in the shape of suppositories – there was plenty of imagination on display. Some drawings were sloppy; others decorated down to the smallest details. One student had gone so far as to draw a frame along the edge of the page. A future gallery curator at work . . .

And that's when she saw it.

Taped above the light switch.

Little Laurie's drawing.

21

She didn't need to read the first name written on the bottom of the page. Mrs Préau recognised the tree with fat tears falling from its branches: the birch. The little girl had made her house look much bigger than it actually was. The windows were ridiculously small, the door askew. A chimney spewed curls of black smoke. The garden was bristling with blades of grass as stiff as sticks. In the left-hand corner of the page, a big orange sun beamed its rays like a hairy belly. But most interesting was how she represented her family: the father and mother were the same size. He was smoking a stick (a cigarette, no doubt), she wore a skirt and a kind of egg-yolk yellow cloche on her head (her hair). Laurie had drawn them in the garden, near where the swing would be. She stood by their side, as big as her mother, holding a pink flower. As for Kévin, he was next to her, symbolised by a circle with two holes (head) and five sticks corresponding to the arms, legs and trunk. Suffice to say that her little brother was of no interest. But what made Mrs Préau shudder appeared in the other part of the garden. Something made up of five sticks and an empty circle.

'You're sure there isn't a third child at the Desmoulins' house? Have a look here . . .'

The headmistress in turn looked closely at the drawing.

'That's strange, yes. I hadn't noticed. It looks like she's drawn something . . . a dog, perhaps?'

'Do you think it looks like an animal?'

The headmistress seemed disconcerted by the discovery too. She would ask Mr Di Pesa tomorrow. Maybe he would know what the little girl had drawn. The headmistress seemed worried as she went back down the stairs.

'Why are you so interested in the Desmoulins family? Is there a problem?'

Caught off guard, the old woman almost missed a step. She clung to the railing. The headmistress took her by the elbow.

'The staircase is a bit steep, be careful.'

'Thank you. I forgot. The Desmoulins family and I are neighbours. We don't know each other very well yet, but the mother asked if I would give extra classes to their son.

109

I thought she was talking about their older son ... Seeing as Kévin is only in the youngest class ... Maybe I misunderstood.'

'I see. Why don't you give me a ring tomorrow at break time at about three? I'll be in my office. I might have the answer about the drawing.'

Mrs Préau thanked the headmistress warmly for the spontaneous visit. On the way back, she walked as fast as she could, holding up the collar of her coat. The sun had disappeared and the cold – or perhaps the excitement – reddened her cheeks.

Notes: Friday 25 September

Called the headmistress at three as agreed.

Got the answering machine three times.

On the fourth attempt, got the expected response: no brother in the Desmoulins family.

Confirmed by the academic records of the two children.

According to her teacher, Laurie would have drawn her 'imaginary friend'.

The teacher asked me to say nothing of my visit to the school. She seems to be afraid of something, but what?

Trust no one.

Even teachers.

On the way back from the Intermarché at five, found a plastic bag full of plums hanging on the gate. A note written on the back of an advertising circular from the Post Office:

'I buried Brutus. But I cannot wash my hair or it will fall out (because of the radiation caused by mobile phones). Thank you for your nice message. I will keep it in mind. Delphine Blanche.'

6.30 p.m. Saw Mr Desmoulins' car back into the garage. No child in the back seat or the front seat.

12.10 a.m. Noises in the attic. Take my 4 mg of Risperdal and also my Stilnox, which will allow me to sleep – the effect is very noticeable.

   Thinking about buying mousetraps.

22

The man stopped short in front of the piano. 'Is this is a Gabriel Gaveau?'

'In walnut veneer. Art Nouveau,' specified Mrs Préau.

'The Sun model. Nineteen twenty-five?'

'Nineteen twenty.'

The piano tuner put his toolbag on the polished floor and approached the instrument slowly. He ran his fingers over the frame and crouched to feel lower down.

'Keyboard on console columns with a carved leaf motif.'

He stroked the double arms, light moving along the piano's feminine curves, and slid his hands into the brass handles, strummed the keys covered in yellowed ivory and then, abruptly, opened the belly of piano. Sitting in the background, her hands folded in her lap, Mrs Préau stared at the piano tuner, a lingering hint of distrust in her heart. She had not appreciated the doorbell ringing an hour ahead of schedule. The tuner had a Breton-sounding name and an Asian face. Which certainly did not improve matters. Mrs Préau only opened her home to people who had clearly identified themselves. The man had to introduce himself, pass his business card through the grille of the gate, explain how he had been adopted by his parents in an orphanage in Cambodia and justify his being early by explaining that a previous appointment had been cancelled before Mrs Préau finally agreed to let him into her home.

'The mechanism is out of tune and dusty, but in good condition.'

He turned to the owner of the premises. 'I'll need at least an hour.'

'Very well.'

'You're going to stay here?'

'Yes, why? Would it bother you?'

'I'm not used to it, that's all.'

'Well, it doesn't bother me. I want to see what you do to my Gaveau.'

He laughed, removing his jacket.

'Nothing too bad. I'm going to try to make it sing in tune, that's all.'

The tuner knew his stuff. That he was an Asian Breton

in Seine-Saint-Denis lent a certain *je ne sais quoi* to the situation. Mrs Préau watched her piano being dusted with a sense of peace. She felt somehow that years of neglect were being taken off of her, too. Hadn't she abandoned the piano, like everything else, without a second thought? It was still the repository of all her secrets; as a child, she had told it everything that grown-ups refused to listen to and that scared the other kids. It was on this piano that she played her first piece for four hands with the future father of her child. Back then, Gérard still had the plump cheeks of a teenager, captivated by his cousin's fantasies, once he got past his initial fear of her. Mrs Préau ended up snoozing in her chair, listening to each hesitant tone find its rightful place, up or down until perfectly in tune. Then the tuner started in on a frenzied version of Handel's *Passacaglia*. The time had come for her to leave her chair and take a few new notes out of her purse that she had withdrawn from the bank the day before.

She was looking forward to tomorrow.

To play for the child who had asked her to.

So long as it doesn't rain.

23

Over his sweatshirt, he had donned a dark blue anorak that was too short. His skinny wrists stuck out of his sleeves. It didn't seem to bother him. He recovered a burst ball and tried to fill it with soil to restore its round shape, scratching his head lazily. The other two children bickered for the swing. Judging this to be the right moment, Mrs Préau put the binoculars down on the table and went to the living room. She opened the curtains and the window, sat down at the piano and began a series of Charles-Louis Hanon exercises, which she knew by heart. She continued with a Czerny study and, having the feeling that she wouldn't go on much longer, she launched into an improvisation, a series of chords with the left hand, against which the right hand picked out a melody. When a moped passed in the street, blocking out the piano with its shrill buzzing, Mrs Préau stopped playing. Her joints were hurting and she was suffering from a bad back. She massaged her fingers and then her neck before getting up. Then she listened. On the other side of the street, Kévin's shouts answered his sister's taunts. Could he have heard the piano from the garden across the way? The old woman went to the window and peered through the cedar foliage behind the latticed concrete wall. Nothing moved in the weeping birch. She stayed like that for several minutes before returning to her room to get the binoculars. Crouching, the boy continued to fill the flat ball with soil and scratch his head. What was she hoping for? That the child would hold up a banner that read 'thank you for the music'? That he'd applaud at the end of the concert? Mrs Préau had no idea. But that there was no change in the child's behaviour affected her so badly that she forgot to eat dinner and went to bed at seven without having washed. In the middle of the night, she was awakened by the passing 2.45 freight train and then by rustling from the attic. As she couldn't get back to sleep, she went to the kitchen to nibble some biscuits and drink a glass of warm milk. She went back to the bathroom to freshen up and to soak the joints in her aching hands, and listened to the pathetic mewing of a cat coming from the garden shed – was some idiot molly there to mourn the one-eyed tom? – then she lay down again.

It was only in the morning, when she opened her bedroom shutters, that she saw it.

The burst ball that the child had filled had landed in her flowerbed.

24

Thursday night dinner had turned into lunch on Mondays at Yakitori Express, a Japanese restaurant. Martin could have taken her to a kebab shop; it would have made no difference. Mrs Préau was in a hurry to finish. The place was noisy, the menu sticky and the food certainly tasteless. But Martin was in the habit of going there. The waitress brought them two overly sweet kirs and prawn crackers, which the medic munched absent-mindedly.

'It's convenient for me here because I'm close to the surgery. That gives us an hour to chat. It's not bad, is it?'

'If you say so.'

Mrs Préau unfolded a paper napkin so thin that it almost flew away.

'So . . . what does one eat here?'

'Raw fish or meat skewers.'

'Raw fish. You're sure?'

'I come here almost every day. I haven't ended up in A&E yet.'

'Yes. Well, I think I'll pass. Have you heard from your father?'

Martin stared into his mother's face. Her features were drawn, her skin dull and slack.

'What's wrong, Mum?'

'What do you mean, what's wrong?'

'Usually, you ask me that question at dessert.'

'Oh? Well, today I wanted a change.'

'Are you sleeping well?'

'Yes. Actually, I have a mouse problem.'

'Mice? Where?'

'In the attic. But don't worry, the problem is about to be sorted.'

Martin swallowed his aperitif in one gulp. He clinked the champagne flute against his mother's.

'You're not drinking your kir?'

'No thank you. You know, I've gone back to the piano—'

The waitress came to take their orders, interrupting Mrs Préau.

'Excuse me, are you ready to order?'

The latter stared at her.

'I feel as if we've met ... Your father isn't a piano tuner, by any chance?'

The young woman looked a bit embarrassed. She was having trouble with the term 'tuner'. Martin half choked on his prawn crackers.

'My mother is making a joke.'

'I think you look very much like him,' continued Mrs Préau.

The waitress nodded and gave a slender laugh, believing it to be a compliment. Satisfied, the old lady put on her glasses and leaned into the menu.

'What do you recommend for the speediest food poisoning, set menu M1 or B13?'

Mrs Préau chose her kebabs according to her son's advice. She told him what she had learned recently about Charcot and Daudet in two biographies borrowed from the library, and expressed her regret that Michel Onfray could publish drivel like *The Aesthetics of the North Pole* or *The Art of Enjoyment*, among other relevant philosophical works; she raged against the hedge-cutters who never stopped ringing the doorbell to offer their services at all hours, and passed quickly over her visit to the Blaise Pascal School.

'You went back there?' gaped Martin. 'They let you in?'

121

'Why not? I am not a terrorist, so far as I know.'

'That's not what I mean. You can't just drop into a school any more. You have to be the parent of a student or have an official reason to go there.'

Mrs Préau took no notice. She moved on to another topic of conversation: Isabelle.

'I'm not sure I want to keep her.'

Martin dropped his chopsticks.

'Don't start this again, Mum. You're not going to make us go through the maid who goes through your things and steals your jewellery rigmarole again. Isabelle is perfect. She has been taking care of the house for years. When you were away—'

'When the cat's away, the mice will play.'

Martin glared into his mother's eyes.

'Let me be clear: if Isabelle goes, you go too!'

'Excuse me?'

'You heard me.'

Leaning towards her, enunciating each word, he said, 'I'll send you to a retirement home.'

Mrs Préau carefully rested her chopsticks on the plastic placemat. The reappearance of her ex-daughter-in-law in her son's life was making itself felt: this was a speech that showed how Martin was being fed hostility towards her. Never underestimate the power of the enemy. She knew it was too early to get rid of the housekeeper. She would get back to that later. For now, there was an important matter to resolve: to learn about the Desmoulins family. She had to get to the bottom of the story of this child who doesn't exist: why is he not in school, and why does his sister deny his existence, while still putting him in her drawings?

'You're still seeing Dr Mamnoue on Wednesdays?' asked Martin.

'Of course.'

'How's it going?'

Mrs Préau straightened, taking on the air of a circumspect headmistress.

'Well, we discuss many different subjects. The lamentable state of public services in the region, for example. Abolishing the business tax represented a loss of three hundred million euros in taxes for Seine-Saint-Denis. And, for now, there is still no compensatory allowance from the state. I am very worried for the future of corporate taxpayers. But you can call him if you want.'

'I will call him. Are you sure you're taking your sleeping pills?'

'Yes, yes, don't worry. All is well. And my blood pressure is good. So long as I don't eat too much of this MSG-tainted food, I shouldn't fade away.'

Despite his age, Martin still needed to be reassured.

Mrs Préau made sure that he was.

She put a hand on his left arm and smiled tenderly.

She did not speak of Bastien, or of the burst ball in her garden.

25

After he dropped her off, Mrs Préau waved at her son from the front porch. The old woman did not open the door. She went back down the steps and closed the gate behind her. A moment later, she was sitting on the number 229 bus. Mrs Préau got off a few steps from 4a Rue Alsace-Lorraine. She was received immediately by Ms Polin, the social worker on duty, a woman in her fifties with skin still tanned from her holidays; an alleged abuse case was a priority.

On the walls of the office where they sat, posters aimed at a public in trouble set the tone for the interview: sordid affairs were handled here. On one of the posters, a baby was pictured sitting in a high chair. His terrified eyes reflected the slogan inscribed under his chair: *The only witness to the domestic abuse of women is often two years old.* AIDS, hepatitis B, illiteracy, paedophilia, violence against women – each image was a slap to Mrs Préau, helpless in the face of so many evils. Leaning on her handbag as she sat on a chair with a grey faux-leather backrest that dug into her middle, she felt the blood pounding quickly in her veins.

'Can you tell me more about this child?'

Name and address of the parents, approximate age and general condition of the boy. Ms Polin noted the details given by her interviewee carefully on a large notepad. Her right hand slipped nervously onto the page. A pendant that matched a pair of cherry earrings shimmered with her movements.

'You say he's not in school?'

'It seems not. His brother and sister are currently in the Blaise Pascal School. The parents have been living in the area for two years, so the child must have been doing his last year of Infants in the same school. But the school headmistress assured me that Laurie and Kévin were the only Desmoulins children to have been registered.'

'You spoke to the headmistress?'

'Very briefly.'

'This doesn't mean that he hasn't been in school: perhaps he's still attending his old school. We would need to know their previous address to check. Have you witnessed any mistreatment of the child?'

Mrs Préau shifted in her seat. The interview was making her uncomfortable.

'I've never really seen him up close.'

'Do you mean to say that you haven't met him?'

Mrs Préau crossed her legs.

'No. But I have been watching him playing in the garden every Sunday for months, and the view from my window is unobstructed.'

Ms Polin raised an eyebrow.

'From your window?'

Mrs Préau pulled at the hem of her black skirt. She had the feeling that she had suddenly crossed over to the wrong side.

'From my window, yes. Listen, I know that an old lady who spies on her neighbours from behind the curtains sounds ... well. But I wouldn't have come to bother you if ... The life of a child is in danger, do you understand?'

The social worker rubbed the top of her pen mechanically with her thumb.

'Madam, may I ask your age?'

'I use binoculars,' answered Mrs Préau weakly.

'I couldn't quite hear you.'

The old woman coughed lightly.

'I use opera glasses. And I hope that your vision is as good as mine when you're over seventy.'

Ms Polin readjusted her garnet-coloured rectangular glasses.

'I think that ship has sailed.'

'Pardon?'

'I'm talking about my prescription,' she said, tapping her frames with a pen before rereading her notes. 'So far, we have an initial witness statement based on an observation of a child of about seven or eight years of age living some thirty metres from your home, a child who never leaves his house and who isn't being educated either. Right. Any other witnesses? Family members? Neighbours?'

Mrs Préau shook her head.

'I live alone. And the part of the garden where the child stays isn't visible from any other house because of the weeping birch tree that his little sister put in a drawing for school – under which you can see the outline of a child.'

'I see. I am going to pass on these details to the CPIO. But I must ask if you would like your name to appear in the file, or if your statement is anonymous.'

'What is the "CPIO"?'

'An office that collects information of concern. It works in conjunction with Child Social Services, based in Neuilly-sur-Marne.'

Mrs Préau refused to let her name and address go on the report on the grounds that she didn't want the neighbours to know that she was the source of the report.

'I don't know them, and I'd be worried about how people might react, you know.'

'That's understandable.'

'How many days will it take for the office you mentioned to process the report?'

'It shouldn't be too long, but don't expect to hear from us any sooner than a month from now if all goes well.'

'A month? But that's frightfully long! What if the child is suffering?'

'We have no choice but to follow procedure. We have to call the parents in with all their family records, and if they don't respond, that can take more time still.'

The social worker stood up: the interview was over. She accompanied Mrs Préau to the lobby and held out a cold hand.

'Well, thank you, Mrs Préau, for coming in to flag up this child's case to us.'

'Could I ring you to find out how things are coming along?' she chanced.

'Of course. But give it a fortnight.'

Mrs Préau left the social welfare centre with a bad feeling. She decided to walk rather than take the bus. She got home at about four. Rain had started to fall, and the garden released the smell of wet earth. She dropped her key twice before sliding it into the lock. She took off her shoes, put the kettle on for tea and then thought better of it. Exhausted, she went up to her room and fell asleep in her slippers without having bothered to draw the curtains.

29 September 2009

For the attention of Roselyne Bachelot
Minister of Health and Sports

Minister,

Please allow me to respond to the scandals erupting in the Church today. I am heartbroken three times over. Heartbroken with shame to think that priests abused children for whom they were responsible, as I myself was responsible, as headmistress of a school, for the outcomes of thousands of students. I am heartbroken with sorrow for the victims whose childhoods were ruined. I am heartbroken as a retired teacher, as to be a teacher is to devote oneself to the education and future of our children.

At some point, the silence becomes unbearable, and people talk. The Church as an institution is confronting it now, but it will not be the only one. I would like to draw your attention, Minister, to the fact that a gym teacher and an Army general were recently arrested.

Paedophilia does not only strike the Church and celibate men. It is often a phenomenon within families, a perversion for which there is no cure.

We talk a lot about the celibacy of priests. This celibacy is often experienced as an amputation, not only in terms of sexuality, but also in emotional terms. Just imagine that these men never hold anyone in their arms; they never feel anyone's arms around them, apart from their immediate family. That is very difficult to live with, believe me. I myself have been divorced since 1975, and, having chosen not to remarry so as to devote myself to my son and my job, I know how it feels. I think of all those men and women who suffer from loneliness and lack affection, and I wouldn't be surprised if some were to plunge into depression, alcoholism or perversity. How many priests leave their parishes to 'rest' when in reality they are in nursing homes to treat chronic depressive conditions? Listening to unhappiness can drown us in it. Personally, I meditate an hour a day.

It seems to me that recognising the emotional want suffered by a great majority of the French population is crucial to the future of our society, which tries to medicalise an emotional problem. I think that if we increased the time dedicated to mutual support, solidarity and the exchange of ideas, we could bring about a reduction in the Social Security deficit. This would be

just that – true 'social security': reassuring the forgotten,
giving them back a place among us, helping them before
they are in distress.

I hope you will hear this appeal from a modest retiree
who no longer expects much from life other than a bit
more time to lend a helping hand to her neighbours.

Respectfully yours,

Elsa Préau

26

For the next week, the old lady watched in horror as a crane was erected behind the Desmoulins family's home. With the residence on Rue des Petits Rentiers nearing completion, work was continuing with the construction of a halfway house opposite the train station. There would be no respite for the residents: dumper trucks and JCBs smashing apart a little more tarmac each day, hollowing out nest-holes in each corner of the Rue des Lilas.

From her room, Mrs Préau had a perfect view of the crane operator perched some fifty metres up. It was a shame he didn't work on Sundays. At that height, the stone boy would have to be in his field of vision. But the presence of this crane would mean that she would have to keep the first- and second-floor shutters closed. Allowing herself to be spied upon so blatantly was out of the question.

And they spoke of practically nothing else at the physio: the construction of the new halfway house. Local residents were concerned about the potentially high-risk population, and were talking about convicts, former drug addicts or alcoholics.

'If I were you, I would take on at least two body-guards,' joked Mr Apeldoorn.

The physio always had a joke for Mrs Préau and worked wonders on her neck. His patient replied that she kept her father's hammer close at hand in case things got rough, and that had amused Mr Apeldoorn, the expression 'in case things got rough'. In the last few weeks, he had been strutting about the place: his weighing scales had been giving him good news.

'That's the Sarkozy diet at work! No bread, no pasta or flour. You have to avoid everything that makes crumbs – but you can have marshmallows and chocolate!'

He also referred to a diet based on lactofermentation, which very much interested his patient.

The Wednesday-afternoon session with Dr Mamnoue was devoted to his patient's telephone. Mrs Préau had been receiving strange phone calls since the school year had begun. The phone rang automatically at 9.20 a.m. and 5.10 p.m. two to three times a week. She would pick up and then hear the voice of a woman she didn't know ask her to 'Please be patient while I connect you to your operator'. Then, without fail, two minutes later, the line would be cut. These calls were bothering Mrs Préau: the automatic message delivered gave her no opportunity to intervene, which led to her being frustrated and angry.

'Have you thought about getting onto the do-not-call list?' asked Dr Mamnoue, examining his sleeves one after another in search of a trace of wear or an ink stain.

'Don't you think that I'm already on the do-not-call list, Claude?'

'Maybe you recently answered a questionnaire on, I don't know, an environmental charter in which you were asked if you intended to change your windows to save energy.'

Mrs Préau's eyes widened.

'I received a letter from the electricity company to which I responded, actually. It was about my insulation and installing double-glazing.'

'Ah! They're very savvy about marketing. It wouldn't surprise me one bit, dear Elsa; this is certainly one of those semi-state partners of the electricity company harassing you with an offer on new windows – a service for which the electricity company gets a small commission, that goes without saying.'

'So it will continue?'

'Without a doubt.'

'I'm going to have to change my number. That's very annoying.'

Dr Mamnoue sat back in his chair and moved on to examine his cufflinks.

'Give it a little time. The calls will probably dry up, or their automated call system will eventually put you in contact with a salesman before disconnecting. These tele-marketing systems are far from fully functional.'

By the end of their conversation, a temporary solution had been found: put the phone off the hook at 9.20 and 5.10. Mrs Préau paid for the session, during which she had been careful not to mention her visit to Ms Polin, the social worker.

On Friday, she did not forget to add a packet of cara-mels to her shopping list. She would need them for an experiment that she had come up with on Thursday when she went to borrow some books from the local library: a brand-new 'tactile' book was waiting for little hands to open it and enjoy the story of *Hansel and Gretel*.

When Ms Briche visited Mrs Préau on Saturday morn-ing, she found that her blood pressure was high. She explained to the nurse that she was immersed in a fascin-ating book by a university professor about rumours, and had read well beyond a reasonable hour last night. As a result, she had doubled her dose of morning coffee. Neither woman believed the lie.

Waiting for news from the social worker and looking

out for any sign of the child in the garden was putting her nerves on edge.

By contacting social services, she had chosen to give up on her peace of mind.

But whatever the price, Mrs Préau was ready to pay it if it could save the child who looked like Bastien.

27

Each weekday, she had done her utmost to work on her fingering. For almost ten years, Mrs Préau had lived surrounded by the elderly, and palm trees, with only the following activities: walking, reading and preparing meals – she never ate in the refectory with the other residents. The baby grand piano in the common room of the home allowed her to keep up practising and avoid lots of chattering sets of dentures. The waiting audience, nestled in velvet club chairs, always hoped that she would play the choruses of songs that would make their hearts leap, hits by Piaf or Yves Montand. To spite her entourage, Mrs Préau would only play pieces by Satie. She had his whole repertoire at her fingertips, 'Pièces froides', 'Préludes flasques', 'Enfantillages pittoresques', 'Rêveries nocturnes', 'Gnossiennes' – such compelling works – and of the six pieces dating from 1906 to 1913, 'Effronterie' was her favourite. By contrast, the 'Gymnopédies' bored her stiff. Yet that was the only piece appreciated by the other residents. As a one-time boarder at private institutions where they had gone to great pains to make a good Christian out of her, she had retained a sense of sacrifice. So the pianist dished up what her audience wanted, year in, year out, like soup in a flavour that surprises no one any more.

Earlier, she had gone to play for the stone boy. And for Bastien, it went without saying. The *concertiste* had the three 'Peccadilles importunes' from Satie's works for children. She thought them appropriate to the mood of the garden, a breeding ground of screaming and bickering. She played them in the order set out by the composer: 'Being jealous of his big-headed friend', then 'Eating his sandwich', and finally 'Taking advantage of the corns on his feet to steal his hoop'.

For now, she had to sort out the caramels. Bastien could not pronounce the word 'caramel' correctly when he was little: in his mouth, the sweet turned into Carabas, suggesting that the sweets came from the distant kingdom of the Marquis from *Puss in Boots*. Smiling at the memory, Mrs Préau put on her coat, tied a pink scarf around her neck, swapped her slippers for a pair of boots and went out into the street, her pockets full of caramels.

There was no one on the path. Briskly, Mrs Préau crossed the street. She leaned against the high concrete wall that shielded the Desmoulins family garden from being overlooked, exactly where, on the other side of the cedar curtain, the little boy would be less than an hour later. The old lady pulled a handkerchief from her pocket. With one hand, she pretended to blow her nose, while she surreptitiously slipped one caramel after another into the lattice of the openwork concrete wall. With their pink and yellow packaging, they would no doubt attract the child's attention. A dozen fell down on the other side beneath the shrubs. Two caramels remained struck in the latticework. Mrs Préau folded up her handkerchief, and returned home.

Later, still decked out in scarf and coat, she would play Satie, as free as a bird with the windows swinging open until the shouts from the neighbouring garden stopped. Then she would climb up to her room, and, binoculars in hand, look for traces of sweet wrappers where the child had last been.

She found nothing.

She looked all over the garden with the binoculars, and saw not a trace of sweet wrappers. Could it be that the child hadn't found the caramels? Yet the boy had been there, crouching near the cedar, she had seen him, dressed in his too-short anorak and shapeless tracksuit bottoms, his face looking drawn and his skin dull.

Unfazed, he lined up twigs and small sticks in front of him. The sticks had been there on the ground, in a mess, a metre from the hedge, spread out in a strange way – almost geometric.

Mrs Préau shivered.

There was a picture laid out on the pale grey gravel with twigs.

Something like a giant caramel.

Notes: Sunday 4 October

Difficult to tell whether this drawing on the ground, the bloodstained stones and the ball filled with soil are signs of an attempt by the child to communicate.

May be simple games or diversions.

Possible, for example, that the stone boy does not have all of his mental faculties, which would explain his submissive attitude, lack of communication with others and his non-attendance at school.

Along the same lines: it could be that the child, suffering from mental disorders, is taken in by an institution during the week and that his parents bring him back for the weekend. And, as it is not uncommon for this type of mental illness to be associated with behavioural disorders such as anorexia and to lead to other deficiencies, the poor overall condition of the stone boy could well be justified.

Increased dose of Stilnox a week ago and sleeping better (more than six hours of sleep per night). But waking is arduous: I have the sensation of floating all day, which makes my reading time more difficult. I also noticed that my muscles feel weak and my usual trips on foot are more tiring. The effect should wear off in time.

Last night, from 10 p.m. to 1, more noises in the attic.

Mouse problem unresolved.

Double the dose.

Notes: Monday 5 October

This morning Isabelle discovered two caramel wrappers rolled into balls on the pavement in front of the gate.
   Forget last night's theory.
   <u>*The child has begun to communicate with me.*</u>

Met Ms Polin this afternoon to tell her the story about the caramels. She promised to make a note in the file. Told me that the letter calling the Desmoulins parents in for a meeting went out at the end of last week. Given the urgency of the matter (abuse and truancy), she sent it to speed things up. The meeting is scheduled for Tuesday 13 October at the social welfare centre.
   I called Martin to cancel lunch (I'm too agitated). My son could hardly hide his joy. Said he still would come here tonight to take my blood pressure. Had got a message on Saturday that the nurse was worried (the bitch). Martin wants to revise plans for my long-term treatment.
   I took a quarter of a Stilnox to be well relaxed if he comes as planned.

DON'T FORGET:

Ask Isabelle to stop cleaning the second floor.
Wait a night before installing traps.
Look for a book on lactofermentation at the library.

28

'Did you ever wonder what my life would have been like if I had had a normal mum?'

Mrs Préau smiled ironically.

'First of all, what is a normal mum?'

Martin pumped the blood pressure cuff. The cuff tightened around his mother's left arm.

'A mother like everyone else's.'

'Oh, right. Common, then.'

'No, a mother who gives a real gift to her son, for example.'

'I take issue with that, Martin. You can't say that I didn't spoil you.'

The cuff shrank sharply. Martin put it back in his bag and pulled out a stethoscope.

'Even the year that Dad left?'

The cold metal touching the base of her neck made Mrs Préau shudder.

'Maybe not that year. I was very unhappy at the time, you know, and I think that I didn't do things the way they ought to have been done.'

'Thank you for telling me that. It's rare for you to acknowledge your mistakes. Giving me a hat and mittens for Christmas, that was bloody lousy. Can you lift up your jumper, please?'

'Oh! Well, your mother isn't perfect, Martin,' replied Mrs Préau, pulling up her top, 'and I've never claimed to be. I grant you that I'm different from other mothers, or at least from the ones I came across during all those years at Blaise Pascal. They all seemed to have been made from the same mould.'

'Now that I would have liked – a mum out of a mould, just like other mums, one who doesn't talk to ghosts.'

'What are you talking about? I've never talked to ghosts. I sometimes hear noises.'

'But you do – I've caught you a few times, talking to yourself, alone in the house, whispering stuff to the sink . . .'

'No. That's just thinking aloud. When you're alone like I am all day long, and there's no one to talk to, then inevitably you start talking to walls, the staircase . . .'

Martin put the stethoscope away.

'You're talking to the staircase now? I wonder what exactly it is you have to say to yourself.'

'Nothing, I'm telling you. Are you doing this on purpose? So I talk to myself. You're annoying.'

'I'm only teasing. You can get dressed . . . '

Martin closed his threadbare bag. It was reassuring to arrive and find his mother calm and relaxed. Contrary to what the nurse had suggested, she was perfectly fine.

'But still – you must admit that to have a mother who devotes her time to other children can be unsettling for a son.'

'Don't confuse things, please. It's true that I gave a great deal of myself to my work. But if I'm not mistaken, your father did too. And it is for that reason that he left.'

'You told him to leave.'

'Yes, no, well, I asked him to choose, it's not the same. Anyway. Do you want something to drink before you go home?'

'No, thank you, I've got to go; I still have house calls to make.'

Martin got up off of the plush sofa. Mrs Préau got up too, pulling her jumper over her long skirt.

'Tell me, son, is the phone number of this house on the do-not-call list?'

'Yes, why? Are you getting calls from telemarketers?'

'It's annoying but I've found a trick. A propos, never

try to reach me at around nine twenty a.m. or five ten. I put the phone off the hook ... Where are you going?'

Martin was about to climb the stairs.

'To my room, why?'

Mrs Préau grabbed a purple wool shawl from the cupboard in the hall.

'Now? But it hasn't been cleaned ...'

'Oh, I'm just going to take two or three books,' he said over his shoulder as he climbed the stairs.

'I'd rather that you didn't go up there today. Because of the mice.'

Martin's voice echoed down the stairs from the first-floor landing: 'Mice? We have mice? Are you sure?' He sounded surprised.

'Yes, Martin, I told you, I think they're hiding in the attic. So I went down to the hardware shop—'

'Good God, Mum, what the hell is this?'

One sharp crack and then another. Martin unleashed a torrent of curses.

'There are at least fifty of them!'

Mrs Préau covered her shoulders with the shawl, defeated. He had reached the second-floor landing. Martin would carry on believing that his mother was losing her mind. She had not been careful.

She should have waited until her son had gone before laying all the traps.

29

On Tuesday, Mrs Préau found it hard to do her stretching exercises. She apologised to Mr Apeldoorn. She explained that her tiredness was caused by the sudden change in the weather: a warmth that viruses loved, turning the flora on its head and disrupting the proper order of things. The constant noise of nearby construction work was also a significant factor.

'It puts your nerves on edge.'

'I want to believe you, Mrs Préau. Bend, push!'

That morning, the old lady had checked the mousetraps. But she had her doubts about what the Pakistani man in the hardware shop had sold her: no harm had come to them. Yet she had heard scratching overhead until five in the morning. Perhaps they didn't fancy the

Gruyère she had cut into pieces and spread out on the traps? Maybe the mice took a different route than up the stairs. Isabelle would have to stop cleaning for a few days and then they could look on the ground and follow the little droppings straight to their hideout, like Tom Thumb.

'How is it possible that my house is full of so many pests when at least five cats, including one pregnant female, come every day to the garden shed to eat? I wonder if I wouldn't be better off catching the cats first, and then releasing them in the attic.'

'You know what Albert Schweitzer said – there are two ways to forget life's worries: music and cats.'

'Sounds more like Michel Tournier.'

'Maybe. I heard it on the telly. Bend, lift. And how did you get on with the lactofermentation diet?'

'I started my jars of carrots, turnips and courgette. You're hurting me, Mr Apeldoorn.'

'Have we decided to be a wimp today? Did you top them up to the brim with brine? Bend!'

On Wednesday morning, the housekeeper had been in a foul mood. She had been muttering as she tied her apron and put on her slippers. She wasn't happy about having to step over mousetraps in order to dust the second floor.

'Leave the dusting on the second floor and concentrate on the other rooms, Isabelle.'

'That isn't logical, Mrs Elsa.'

'Logical? Because there's a logic to how the cleaning is done now?'

Isabelle leaned on her broom and sighed drily.

'If I cannot clean upstairs, it'll come down the stairwell. Dust flies about the place, Mrs Elsa.'

Later, the phone rang. It was neither 9.20 nor 5.10. The schedule for the automatic calls had changed, and the line crackled loudly. 'Do not hang up; your call is being answered by one of our representatives who will be alerted to your call by a beep.' Soft music followed, accompanied by an advertisement that highlighted the significant energy savings to be made by a well-insulated house. Exasperated, Mrs Préau finally unplugged the phones in the living room and bedroom.

30

On Wednesday, leaving her house to go to Dr Mamnoue's, the old lady noticed some droppings on the paving stones between the front steps and the gate. A pair of blue tits had taken up residence in the large ash tree. She thought it was a promising sign, and an incentive to hold out until Sunday. Not having seen the stone boy for ten days was weighing on her mind. She never would have imagined that time could pass so slowly and that the hours would grind against each other to spite her impatience. At night, Mrs Préau had started to dream again. Her dreams were circus acts. Mice rode astride one-eyed cats; Mr Apeldoorn writhed about in a jar of brine; Dr Mamnoue, dressed as a clown, walked around the floor with a big 'wrong way' sign, holding the hand of a naked woman; her son Martin was in tears holding candyfloss; and in the middle of the tent, Bastien juggled pebbles in a pool of blood.

'Don't you want us to talk about something other than your phone and this lactofermentation diet?' Dr Mamnoue said with a sigh.

The question surprised Mrs Préau.

'What should I be telling you, Claude?'

'About your dreams, for example.'

'I told you: I don't dream any more since I started taking sleeping pills.'

'And the child?'

'The child?'

'Your neighbours' child; do you still see him in the garden?'

Mrs Préau leaned against the back of the chair where she sat at each session. She would have to give him something.

'An investigation is ongoing.'

'Oh, right. So this is serious, then? You contacted social services?'

'Yes. The parents have been called in.'

Dr Mamnoue scratched his left temple.

'Ah! Good. Are you absolutely sure?'

'Do you mean am I sure that the child is being abused? I am certain of it.'

The man shook his head.

'You'll keep me informed?'

'Of course. It also works well with Swiss chard and radishes.'

'What works with Swiss chard?'

'Lactofermentation. You put them in a jar of brine for two or three days in the refrigerator. It doubles the enzymatic potential of the vegetables.'

Dr Mamnoue gave a chuckle.

'First it was gravel, now it's vegetables in jars. Luckily there aren't jars big enough to fit me!'

Mrs Préau smiled back.

'Who could have the daft idea of pickling you, Claude?'

9 October 2009
Care of his publisher
for the attention of Mr Pascal Froissart,
Paris VIII teacher and author

Sir,

I have just finished reading your book about rumours.
You make the distinction between history and fantasy.
You claim that the Internet plays the role of both
memory and distributor but that it does not create
rumours. I think that the Internet is the most monstrous
invention that man has ever created. Our worst fantasies
are found there. It is the largest vehicle of perversity.
Having a computer in my home is out of the question.
For that matter, I have always refused to get a Minitel.
*   You also say that you do not know how to stop*
rumours. Sociologically speaking, the more you deny it,
the more the rumour will spread, and the greater the
number of people who will still doubt you. Of course.
Nevertheless, I think that the rumours that are
circulating currently about our President are carefully

orchestrated and have one sole goal: to instil in the people an image of a man who could be undermined. Believe me, Mr Froissart – and this is not a rumour but a statement of fact – that man is the opposite of chaos. And he knows how to play this apparent mess. There is even a diet named after him, you know: 'the Sarkozy diet, the only crumb-free diet!' Don't you think that we are in the presence of an absolute master in the art of spreading rumours? Imagine the sympathy he can get from followers of this miraculous regime! (I do mean a nutritional regime, you understand.)

Looking forward to hearing from you.

Respectfully yours,

Elsa Préau

31

Since Saturday, hundreds of exhibitors had filled the pathways of Courbet Park to sell and offer tastings of wines, local produce and crafts. The Harvest Festival lasted two days. It had started yesterday at around three o'clock with a parade through the streets of the town. A country wagon pulled by two oxen, a wine tanker decorated with barrels and drawn by four more beasts, barrel-rollers, a cart pulled by a horse, a herd of goats and goat dogs, line dancers and gastronomic and oenological societies from across France had left the East Stadium, and continued along Rue Jean Bouin to reach the park. There an idle crowd waited for the float bearing the Harvest Queen and her Crown Princess. All of the great and the good from the town were there, and perhaps even the County Council.

The Desmoulins family went on Saturday in their Sunday best. Mrs Préau had seen them leaving the house in good spirits, the two youngest kids running up Rue des Lilas. Laurie and Kévin had probably gone to the old-fashioned grape-pressing demonstrations, eaten sausages and chips from the concession stands, enjoyed the amusements and asked for a pony ride. Maybe they had crossed paths with Bastien and his parents at the societies stand?

Mrs Préau would not get to taste the 2008 vintage from the municipal vineyard at the Clos Hills Brotherhood stand. She had headaches and a natural distrust for such popular events and anything that involved petticoats. The stone boy must be unaware of such festivities; maybe he'd never been on a carousel. He would be entitled to his Sunday outing in the garden, no more, no less, and his little legs would take him no further than the weeping birch.

That is where Mrs Préau found him, as she had in previous weeks, a dark miracle that upset her. His head had been shaved, and carelessly. Odd, whitish patches of skin appeared where angles of his skull showed through. His sunken eyes ringed with mauve stared at the cedar leaves. Curled into himself, the boy stood motionless, his head tilted to one side, neglecting to play with his dirt and twigs.

A hoarse cough shook his slender body.

The stone boy was sick and seemed shrivelled like dried fruit.

With a heavy heart, Mrs Préau set down her binoculars; to stop looking at him was to deny him her support, to abandon him to his fate. He didn't look up at her house once. It was a bad sign. She had to act fast: she had to make contact with him. The old lady went downstairs to the living room, opened the windows and got settled at the piano, her shawl over her shoulders. Prelude, interlude and the finale of *Jack in the Box*.

She felt no satisfaction in playing, even though she was giving it the attention and energy that the interpretation required. How could Erik Satie's *Fantasies* comfort a child in such distress? When she let the fingers of her left hand find the first, comforting chords of 'Gnossienne', someone rang the doorbell. Mrs Préau waited for the bell to ring a second time before getting up and walking, stiff-backed, to the front door. When she appeared on the porch, she looked like a child about to be scolded for making too much noise playing her drum set.

32

'Hello! Sorry to bother you ...'

The man who stood at the gate added, 'I'm your neighbour', but it wasn't necessary. Mrs Préau recognised Mr Desmoulins' balding brush of blond hair. Adjusting her shawl, she went down the few steps to meet him. The man smiled, friendly-looking behind the grille.

'I interrupted your concert!' he apologised.

'Not to worry. Let me open this for you.'

Mrs Préau took a key ring out of her pocket and unlocked the gate warily. She had insisted to the social worker that her name not be mentioned in the file, but you never knew what to expect from someone employed by the County Council. The man had something of the military about him despite his casual attire. Thick neck, square chin, beefy shoulders – he looked like he was built to carry bags of cement.

'My wife insisted,' he said. 'It was her idea. But I haven't introduced myself . . . '

His voice was coarse and nasal. He crushed her right hand. A slight smell of frying emanated from his clothes.

'Philippe Desmoulins. And this is our little Laurie.'

The girl stood hidden behind her father's legs, clinging to his tracksuit bottoms.

'Come on, haven't you given up on your shy routine?'

The man caught the little girl by the arm and pushed her in front of him.

'Say hello to the lady. We're here because of you.'

Laurie gave Mrs Préau a nasty look.

The old lady felt as if she had run all the way from the station to the bakery. Her heart began to beat so hard that the blood rushed to her face.

There was no doubt about it: Laurie *knew*.

She had probably seen her in the window on Sunday. She had seen her brother throw stones into her garden, guessed their little game and maybe even found a caramel behind the cedar hedge. Had she told her parents? And had they made the connection with being called in by the social worker? What if Mr Desmoulins came to worm it out of her before settling the score? *If it's that old bitch neighbour who sold us out, she's a dead woman!*

162

The man looked up to the roof, blinking. His blond eyelashes were almost transparent.

'You have a very beautiful house, madam. What year was it built?'

Mrs Préau squeezed the key ring against her chest. She had not thought of this. She had not imagined that she would find herself in this situation. A soft autumn light washed over the garden plants, the leaves took on amber glints and the hydrangeas shook their brocaded petals once again.

It was a perfect day to meet a bad end. Prepared for the worst, Mrs Préau leaned down to the child.

'1908. Hello, Laurie.'

33

They had not come about the stone boy. They were there about the piano. Mrs Desmoulins had heard at the chemist's near the station that there was a lady living on Rue des Lilas who had once given musical theory lessons. She had decided that it could only be Mrs Préau, whose little Sunday-afternoon concerts were so appreciated. So, she had given her husband the job of asking if Laurie could be one of her students.

Mrs Préau nearly died. She composed herself. She apologised for her slightly chilly welcome, justifying herself by explaining that she instinctively distrusted anyone she didn't know ringing the doorbell. She said that she did indeed know the Pommier's chemist where she was occasionally a customer – appreciating as she did their range of compression stockings and socks. She hesitated before inviting Mr Desmoulins and his daughter into her home, but she had no choice: entering into their game was the only logical option.

'I would like to evaluate Laurie's level before giving my answer.'

While the girl perched on the piano stool playing the first notes of some nursery rhymes, Mrs Préau served her father a coffee, which he knocked back – black, no sugar. They talked about the neighbourhood and the building site, about how not all the houses on the street were connected to the sewage mains, the problems caused by the alternating parking system and the lack of double-glazing on Mrs Préau's windows.

'I can get you a good price if you're interested. I work at Lapeyre. I do the installations.'

'What are the chances,' the old lady replied sarcastically.

'It would be less noisy; and warmer in the winter, that's for sure.'

'Maybe I will do it one day. A little more coffee?'

They agreed on a price for the lessons that Mrs Préau would give to Laurie each Wednesday morning, with payment due monthly on the first of the month. As she was leaving, the girl gave a hint of a smile without dropping her sullen demeanour. In fifteen minutes on the piano stool, she hadn't stopped sighing and fidgeting, scratching the top of her thigh or wiping her nose on the sleeve of her blouse. She certainly had no desire to learn the piano. It was already a lost cause. But if Mrs Préau engineered things carefully, Laurie might agree to hand over some horrible family secrets.

Of this she was quite certain.

No child had ever resisted her baking.

Notes: Tuesday 13 October
(Day of the Desmoulins' meeting at the social welfare office)

2.50 a.m. – Awakened in the night by the sound of a coat hanger falling on the floor of my room. Found hanger 30 centimetres from the bed. Impossible to explain how it could get there when it was hanging on a fixed hook behind the door almost two metres away. Great trouble getting back to sleep before dawn. The hissing noise above my head at night is still there. Not a single mouse down.

Talked to my chemist about my health concerns. The floating sensation and muscle weakness I've been having for several weeks are related to mixing Risperdal and Stilnox. I do not want to stop taking the sleeping tablets. My little anxieties are related to lack of sleep, nothing else. I decided to stop the Risperdal as I don't see the need for it at the moment.

Finally solved the problem of the housekeeper: she decided herself not to go up to the second floor any longer. She said it stinks because of the toilets and bad smells that are coming up from the septic tank and also because I keep the windows and shutters closed on the upper floors. No need to open my house to the crane operator who spends his time looking into my garden and spying on what I get up to.

Hugged my ABCs of Rhythm and Notation with glee when I found it in a cardboard box of sheet music in the attic. Stuck the red cover back on with tape.

6 p.m. – Chocolate Swiss roll finally finished. Perfect icing. Must think to wet the tea towel more thoroughly next time for the unmoulding stage.

TO DO:
Start emptying Martin's room. Take his books down and put them in the library in the living room.

   Buy a metronome.

34

Mrs Préau had been wrong. The girl put her heart into it. Her desire to learn the piano was not an act. Held with a fuchsia band, her ponytail swung from one shoulder to the other. Her palms kept time slightly off the beat. Though weak, she played well. Sitting to the left of her teacher, the little blonde girl followed the notes along the stave cut out of cardboard that Mrs Préau moved gently from one line to another, replacing the Fs with Gs. She kept patting the little girl on the back so that she would sit up straight and stop swinging her nervous little feet before they bashed into the piano.

'Yes, Laurie. Bravo. You know your notes already.'

Mrs Préau was getting back into the swing of things. She had not had a student for many years. She had put on a striped purple and white shirt, a cashmere pencil skirt and patent leather ankle boots. Every summer when Bastien was still a baby, she would organise a recital at her house and invite her pupils and their parents. They would blithely push the furniture out of the way and put up garden chairs. In their Sunday best, their hands clammy from fright, pianists would play their favourite works, and a snack would be served in the garden under the plum trees laden with fruit. Mrs Préau served orange juice, lemonade and cakes she had made the night before for her students – vanilla- or lemon-flavour, or stuffed with pieces of dark chocolate. Everyone left with a bag of sweets and rolled-up sheet music clutched to their chests.

'Good. That's enough work. Are you hungry?'

Ten o'clock was the ideal time to lay a trap for a little girl. Mrs Préau led her into the kitchen and sat her down in front of a fat slice of chocolate Swiss roll.

'Enjoy, Laurie.'

Her first spoonful was immediately followed by a second.

'Are you thirsty?'

The girl nodded. While Mrs Préau prepared a glass of cordial for her, she looked up from her plate.

'Mum never makes cake.'

'Oh? That's a shame.'

'Yes.'

'Do you like it?'

'Yes.'

'If you want, you can take home a piece for your brother Kévin.'

'Maybe.'

'And for your imaginary friend, too.'

Laurie grabbed with both hands the glass her teacher had filled.

'I don't have an imaginary friend.'

Standing next to the table, Mrs Préau put the water jug back down, coughing.

'Really? I was sure you did.'

'No way,' said the little girl with a chocolaty smile, 'I'm not a baby any more! It's little babies who have imaginary friends.'

'So it's your brother's.'

'What?'

'It's your brother Kévin who has an imaginary friend.'

'Kévin doesn't have an imaginary friend. He just has a blanky that smells horrid.'

Mrs Préau sat next to the child. Something about Laurie was touching. Her surly, outspoken side revealed an interesting personality. Like a valve on a pressure cooker, she must exhaust her authority over her little brother – the steam vent – and thus obscure the tragedy of the elder brother. Her dreams must be on a par with Mrs Préau's nightmares.

'Would you like to hear a little story?'

Crossing her legs under her skirt, the former teacher began her tale of an old lady whose parents had long since gone up to heaven, and she was unhappy as could be, for she had neither a child nor a husband, nor brother or sister.

'She had no one with whom to share her sorrows and joys. Then, she invented an imaginary friend, made out of salt, water and breadcrumbs, whom she could always count on, like a husband or a big brother.'

'Big brothers are no good,' Laurie interjected.

'Why?'

'They make everyone unhappy.'

'Really? What a funny idea. Why?'

Her little feet bounced under her chair. The girl carefully wiped her mouth.

'Because they're naughty.'

'Naughty? What do you mean, naughty?'

Laurie grabbed her ponytail and twisted it around her fingers.

'Um, naughty is when you make Dad angry all the time. I'd like to go home now.'

The child was visibly uncomfortable. Mrs Préau cleared away her plate.

'Of course, Laurie. I'll walk you home.'

35

Mrs Préau helped the little girl into a horrible pink coat and threw a shawl over her own shoulders. At the gate, the child noticed droppings on the ground, looked up at the ash for something that would pass for a nest and wondered how birds produced so much poo.

'Your garden is beautiful,' she added.

'Thank you, Laurie, but you know, it's a lot of work.'

'Our garden isn't beautiful. There're no flowers.'

'Of course there are, Laurie. There's you.'

The girl seemed to appreciate the metaphor, and took Mrs Préau's hand to cross the street. It was a bit sticky and warm, a feeling that reminded the old lady of her little walks hand in hand with Bastien on Wednesdays and

Saturday afternoons. She wanted to squeeze the little girl's fingers, but held herself back.

'I'll tell you a secret, Laurie: a long time ago, I was a teacher in your school.'

'Really?'

'It's true. And I have seen plenty of students, believe me. Small brothers and big brothers. Nice ones, and not-so-nice ones too. But never naughty.'

'I know loads of naughty ones at school.'

They were standing in front of the lattice concrete wall where Mrs Préau had slipped the caramels. Laurie ran her fingers along it, exactly where caramels were stuck ten days before.

'There were sweets here once,' she said.

Mrs Préau started: could it be that Laurie ate the caramels intended for her brother? How awful. There was a grinding noise. Mrs Desmoulins was standing at the gate of her house with an icy smile. Rather thin, with her hair gathered in a turban, she wore trousers and a cardigan pulled around a sky-blue polo neck that matched her eyes. Laurie dropped her teacher's hand to sidle up behind her mother and cling to her legs. She took a step back.

'Hello. So how did my daughter get on?' she asked, worried.

'Yes, very well.'

'Oh, so much the better!' she said, already about to close the door.

'Laurie has a real musical sensibility.'

'Oh! Well! Wow . . .'

Mrs Préau longed to know whether the Desmoulins had gone to the meeting with the social worker yesterday. She could not help glancing up towards the house. There, behind a door, under a staircase or even in a cupboard, the stone boy was being kept, under strict orders not to make any noise. Behind the house, the crane from the building site stood, imperious. With all the racket, it was unlikely that anyone would hear a call for help. The scaffolding was now higher than the Desmoulins' roof.

'That blasted building site,' said Mrs Préau.

'Oh! It's hellish.' Mrs Desmoulins smiled. 'Fortunately, we had all the windows double-glazed.'

The double-glazing again. Suddenly, the crack in her neighbour's icy smile turned to a grimace. Mrs Préau shuddered: she had seen it before, in between two blows of the hammer.

'Did you hear that?' she said.

'Hear what?'

'It was like a child's cry.'

'Really?'

'Yes, like a stifled moan.'

'Sorry, no . . .'

Laurie chanced a peek at her piano teacher from behind her mother's legs. She had taken on a sullen, almost hostile attitude. Mrs Préau was not going to be let past the gate.

'Ah. It must be coming from the site, then,' said the old lady.

'Yes, I think so. Excuse me, I— I'm right in the middle of tidying up ... Thank you very much for Laurie. Goodbye, madam.'

'Have a good day.'

Crossing the street to go home, Mrs Préau suddenly felt very cold. A strong breeze had picked up and the ash branches whipped the air.

That night, a storm went through Seine-Saint-Denis. Advertising hoardings were blown off the edge of the bypass, the blue tits' nest fell out of the tree and Martin had to go urgently to his mother's bedside.

36

The diagnosis left little room for doubt. Mrs Préau had all the symptoms of influenza A. Martin gave his mother Paracetamol to bring down the fever. He decided to spend the night by her side, sitting in the armchair, having a conversation with Audrette by text.

Mrs Préau had been refusing all vaccines for years. Even though her son shared her doubts about routine immunisation – which did nothing if not keep the pharmaceutical companies happy – he regretted that this year, given the threat of H1N1 virus, his mother had not given in. He feared that she would soon pay a serious price.

With joint and muscle pain and headaches, Mrs Préau was soon too weak to get up and eat anything other than vegetable soup. Martin visited her several times a day, making the round trip in between house calls. He dreaded the onset of a cough and sore throat, signs that it was worsening, which would require antivirals.

'I don't want to go to hospital, Martin,' Mrs Préau murmured in her son's ear whenever he leaned over her to straighten her pillow.

'I know, Mum, I know.'

'You know they'll kill me in hospital. They have instructions. They killed your grandfather, Martin. They gassed him, like my mother.'

'Calm down. Nobody is going to die. And you're not going anywhere for the moment.'

At night, at the height of the fever, Mrs Préau was talking in her sleep, waking up her son – meaningless sentences punctuated by exclamations. *Leave me alone* and *oh no, shit* on a constant loop. Martin fell in and out of sleep in the armchair. Sleeping sitting up was bad for his back, but watching over his mother's health was his duty. He intended to take up his burden, his torments, whatever the sacrifice.

By Friday morning, Martin's resolve was wavering. The fever wasn't going down and Mrs Préau looked smaller under the burning sheets. If in a few hours the patient's condition hadn't improved, they would be forced to go to the hospital. The housekeeper relieved Dr Préau from nine to noon, and then it was the turn of the nurse, Ms Briche, to stay at the sick woman's bedside for another four hours. She kept the fever under control and checked her pulse while doing her crossword magazine, not forgetting to keep the old lady hydrated.

At almost seven o'clock, Martin found his mother sitting up in her bed, her shawl over her shoulders and a book by Virginia Woolf on her knees. She smiled at him. 'You ate?' Martin gawped, discovering on the nightstand the remains of a snack of crackers, cheese and apple.

'I was hungry, yes. So, did you hear them?'

Martin sat on the bed next to his mother.

'What are you talking about?'

'Well, the mice. You've been sleeping in the armchair here for three days, haven't you? You must have heard them.'

The doctor pulled out the stethoscope.

'I don't know; I didn't pay attention. The fever has subsided, it seems ...'

Martin withdrew his hand from his mother's forehead.

'Who made you something to eat?'

'I did, why?'

'You got up?'

'Yes. You said it yourself, the fever subsided.'

Martin sighed. 'Mum, you are still very weak. This morning I was this close to taking you to the hospital. You mustn't get up if there's someone right here to help you. Could you turn towards the window? I'd like to listen to your lungs.'

The old woman obeyed, bending her back.

'But I'm doing very well, son. I wouldn't run a marathon or climb a ladder to prune the plum trees. But going to the toilet or downstairs to the kitchen is well within my capabilities. So you're saying that the mice have kept quiet since Wednesday?'

'Mum, can we talk seriously? You are very sick. Even if you feel like you're getting better ...'

'I am better.'

Martin moved the chest piece of the stethoscope to various points on the patient's back, listening to the sound of her breath.

'It's possible that you have caught a mild form of the flu. But a relapse is likely. Whatever it is, you're contagious, so you'll be confined to the house.'

'But, my shopping, who's going to do that? And I have to take my books back to the library!'

'You can make a shopping list for Isabelle.'

'You know that Isabelle can only read Portuguese.'

'Fine. Then I'll do your shopping.'

'That's nice of you, Martin, but nobody can do my shopping but *me*. I only buy certain products, particularly organic ones.'

'You'll make me a list.'

'Look, I think I have enough supplies to last a few days.'

'Breathe deeply, please.'

Mrs Préau complied. She had difficulty breathing, which led to a little cough. Her son sighed again.

'Mum, I want you to limit how much you move about in the house when you're alone. I'll ask Isabelle to come and prepare your meals for a few days. By the way, I reconnected your phone.'

'Don't you think you're making too much of this?'

Martin raised his hand for silence. He listened to Mrs Préau's heartbeat. Then he crossed his arms, and his shoulders slumped.

'This morning, I hospitalised a little girl who was on the verge of exhaustion. She was choking because of an excess of fluid. Her lungs are severely infected, and she's suffering a great deal. The girl is being treated. I think that she'll get through it, but there will be lasting effects on her respiratory system.'

Unable to find a comeback, Mrs Préau slipped her book under her pillow and straightened her shawl, leaving Martin to take her blood pressure.

'Have you noticed the strange smell in your house?'

'A smell?'

'Yes, it smells like sewage ... Have you been treating the septic tank with bags of Eparcyl? Isabelle told me that you keep the shutters closed on the first and second floors all the time. We have to let the sun and air into your house, Mum – otherwise you'll get sick again.'

While he inflated the cuff around her skinny arm, Mrs Préau prayed that the stone boy didn't have swine flu, and that if he did, he might end up in A&E if his illness got worse. She wondered if the Desmoulins parents did go to the social welfare centre last Tuesday, and then, without warning, she coughed so hard she gave herself a headache.

Notes: Saturday 17 October

Do they beat him? Is it only the father? Is the mother pretending she doesn't know? How can parents inflict such torture on such a young human being, their own flesh and blood? How can you live with this going on next to you? What crime has he committed?

The cough isn't going away.

I don't know how long I'll be in quarantine.

Martin was right about a relapse.

And about the smell.

My house smells bad.

Despite the septic tank treatment.

Find a solution that doesn't require me to open the windows during the day.

Notes: Sunday 18 October

The stone boy appeared in the garden later than usual. His health isn't improving. He's having trouble walking.

Martin is angry at me. I was playing the piano with the windows open when he arrived. Asked me if I wanted to die. I told him that I was playing the piano for Bastien and that he would hear it better if I opened the windows. My answer had an effect: he relented immediately and spoke to me tenderly.

Martin thinks I'm losing my grip.

He asked me if I was keeping up with my therapy.

He'd be better off being wary of Audrette.

I am a miserable woman in a world of misery, but I'm not crazy.

Attempted to contact Ms Polin several times to no avail. This waiting is unbearable. I'm obsessed with the stone boy. At night, I hear him breathing behind the curtains, his moans reach me from the stairwell, and sometimes in the kitchen, I find Bastien with his little baker's apron, cheeks and hands covered with flour. He whispers to me: 'Play for me, Granny Elsa, play for me.'

Drink herbal teas recommended by Dr Mamnoue and continue Stilnox.

Positive point: smell problem resolved with simple stoppers reinforced with pieces of old bath towels.

37

From Sunday night to Monday morning, Mrs Préau didn't say a word. The sleeping tablet she had taken with a glass of green apple liqueur in the evening triggered a breakdown. She meticulously noted the worrying noises in the house – crackling, whispers and other hissing sounds – broke the lead in her pencil three times, and twice went to drink milk in the kitchen where Bastien was waiting for her, silently, sitting on a stool. She collapsed on her bed at 5 a.m., exhausted from coughing. At eight thirty, the jangling of pneumatic drills resumed on the building site. Mrs Préau went downstairs to heat up a cup of coffee. Bastien was not in the kitchen any more. The phone rang at nine.

'Ms Polin here. Could you come in to see me this

morning? What I want to talk to you about cannot be said over the telephone.'

The urgency of the meeting and Ms Polin's nervousness were worrying. What had she discovered? An hour later, the old lady was in the social worker's office, her heart thumping.

Mrs Préau had skipped her morning wash, hastily pulling on a long skirt and polo neck. With her feet toasty in her lined boots, and a purple wool-knit beret covering her grey hair, she took the bus despite Martin's warnings. The fate of the stone boy was worth a citywide flu epidemic.

Ms Polin was not alone in her office with the cheery posters. A permed colleague stood beside her, her arms folded across a sage-green suit.

'Ms Plaisance, a psychologist here at the social welfare centre, and I wanted to inform you as agreed on the results of the meeting with the Desmoulins family ... '

The parents had indeed appeared at the social welfare centre on the allocated day, equipped with their family records.

'The problem is that they do not have a third child.'

The record book proved it. The news hit like a flan hitting a tile floor. Mrs Préau blinked. A computer hard drive under the desk buzzed, making the ground vibrate.

'Surely there must be some mistake. Perhaps it's a question of a child from a previous marriage? In that case, it makes sense that it doesn't appear in the records.'

'I made enquiries to that effect, which is why I did not respond to your calls right away. But neither spouse is divorced. Neither the father nor the mother has another child.'

Mrs Préau shrank into her seat, the victim of a coughing fit. She pulled out a handkerchief from her purse, apologising. The social worker crossed her fingers over the file in front of her.

'What we want to understand, Ms Plaisance and myself, is your reason for contacting us.'

Mrs Préau straightened. She understood immediately where the social worker was going.

'We do not fully understand why you took this approach.'

'I simply came to report a case of abuse. What is the problem?'

'But, Mrs Préau, how can a child be abused who does not legally exist?'

'But he exists, I assure you! I saw him just like I'm seeing you now – it was only last Sunday! And I can assure you that his health has deteriorated significantly in a few weeks.'

The two women exchanged glances. The psychologist put her hands on either side of the desk and leaned forward with a cold smile. The old lady was on her guard.

'Mrs Préau, I understand that you live alone.'

'Yes, that's correct.'

'Forgive me for asking you this question, but do you struggle with loneliness?'

'I'm used to it. It's not a problem for me.'

'But to not have a family, children or grandchildren to hug and to play in your garden, must make you sad, no?'

'I see exactly what you're insinuating. And the answer is no.'

The social worker took over: 'This kind of step is not a small matter, Mrs Préau. By filing a report about this family, you have interfered with the private life of Mr and Mrs Desmoulins, which could cause them problems.'

'Do you have any reason to be annoyed with your neighbours?' added the psychologist.

'Not at all. I don't even know these people!'

'Really? Because they have told us that you were going to give piano lessons to their daughter.'

So there it was.

They were closing in on her.

'How do you know that? Did you speak to them about me?'

'Of course not. We only asked them about their interactions with the neighbours.'

Mrs Préau didn't believe a word of it.

They were in cahoots with the Desmoulins!

The rumble of the computer became more threatening.

What had she expected? Social welfare was part of

189

the County Council. All this was only the next logical step.

Mrs Préau felt herself pale. She was suffocating in this room; it was too dark, too full of aggressive and violent images for her to face these two harpies. The psychologist's steel-blue eyes reminded her of a teacher at the boarding school where her father had sent her against her will. She had a face like tanned leather, with a velvety voice and matchstick legs.

'Listen, I stand by what I said to you. There is a child in a very bad way in my neighbours' garden. If you don't believe me, well, fine, I'll go to the police to file a complaint.'

'We want to believe you, Mrs Préau,' replied the curly-haired psychologist, 'but without proof, it is very difficult. It would have to be proven that the child really does exist.'

Mrs Préau stood and nervously buttoned up her coat. She couldn't wait to leave.

'You only have to come to my house next Sunday, ladies. I'll make you a nice cup of tea and lend you my binoculars. It's crazy how many little details you can see with those binoculars. You can see much further than a family's records, and well beyond the end of your own nose,' she added before leaving the room without closing the door.

As before, Mrs Préau preferred to walk rather than take

the bus. Her hands were trembling. She took Rue Parmentier with the notion to stop at the police station but
changed her mind. The old lady had a migraine setting
in. Better to regain her strength before entering the lion's
den. This battle would be a tricky business – given Mrs
Préau's history.

38

Martin received a call from his mother late in the morning. She asked him if there weren't a more effective cough syrup than Helicidine, and if he could get her a camera that was easy to use. Martin questioned her about what had prompted her to start taking photographs at more than seventy years of age. She said that she wanted to photograph the present to keep track of the truth, rather than live in the past, which Martin took as a tremendously positive impulse and a step on the road to recovery.

'Well, you know, something that's easy to handle, but that can take sharp pictures up to thirty metres.'

Martin promised to take care of it this week. He added: 'Look after yourself, and most importantly, no more open-air piano performances. If the fever doesn't return, you can go out on Friday to do your shopping.'

Mrs Préau hung up with a sigh. She had an adorable son. Too bad he shared his life with a demon.

After having checked all the windows and doors of the house next door through the shutters of her bedroom window, the old lady spent the afternoon on the lookout for the slightest movement in her neighbours' garden.

Mrs Desmoulins went out twice. Wearing a blue fleece and white jeans, she had a mobile phone stuck to her right ear and was pacing the terrace. She left the house at 4.20 p.m. Twenty minutes later, Mrs Desmoulins was back with Laurie and Kévin. All three of them went straight into the house. The shutters on the four windows were closed at six thirty, plunging the house into darkness. However, thanks to the glass bricks arranged above the French doors of what must have been the living or dining room, Mrs Préau could tell whether the light was on or off inside. At about seven o'clock, Mr Desmoulins drove his metallic red Kangoo into the garage. The old lady took the opportunity to take a break from her stake-out. She warmed up a Tetra Pak of organic leek and potato soup, ate two slices of bread she thawed under the grill along with a piece of Comté, and finished off her meal with some Muscat grapes and the France 3 evening news. An item on computer viruses and more specifically the microchips implanted in dogs and cats caught her attention. She promised herself to look up a book in the library that specialised in this area when she was feeling better. If a cat's microchip could 'crack' a computer code simply by the animal being present in the room, millions of people could have been under surveillance without their knowledge and had their privacy violated continuously. At least dogs are forbidden in nuclear power plants. Regardless, from now on, she'd be more wary of stray cats in the garden.

At nine thirty, she had a wash. Then she put on her nightgown, buttoned her woollen coat over it, put on her beret and went to her room, plunged into darkness. She grabbed the binoculars and resumed her post at the window, hidden behind the shutters. Mr Desmoulins came out a quarter of an hour later to smoke. As usual, he had his mobile phone in his hand and seemed very absorbed in it. He was probably playing one of those card games that Martin had shown her in his office; Mrs Préau's son sometimes enjoyed a game of backgammon on his Nokia. But there was no way of knowing for sure. Maybe it was one of those new monitoring tools that allow you to see and hear at a distance. Could Mr Desmoulins be quietly scanning Mrs Préau's house?

The door opened and Mrs Desmoulins appeared wearing her white trousers. She went over to her husband and they exchanged a few words. From where she was with the window open, in the still of the night, Mrs

Préau could only hear a faint murmuring carried on the breeze. The father and mother seemed like conspirators, whispering to each other. Mr Desmoulins even slipped a hand under his wife's jumper. She heard them giggling. Mrs Préau imagined that she was the butt of their jokes. The Desmoulins must have been happy with the trick that they had pulled with the help of the two bitches at the social welfare centre. Soon, a small child's cry rang out from the house. The mother immediately broke away from her husband, looking distinctly displeased, and went back inside, closing the door on the echo of a new cry.

Mrs Préau took a deep breath and rested the binoculars on the side table.

It could well be Kévin.

Or Laurie.

The two bitches at the social welfare centre had been right. Other than the little girl's drawing and the stone boy's appearance on Sundays, to which she was the only witness, nothing could suggest that anything was amiss in this family.

The light was still shining at the neighbours' after midnight. Mrs Préau did not wait for them to turn it off before going to bed. As she still wasn't asleep by the time the freight train passed, disturbed by her cough, she took a glass of green apple liqueur, a big spoonful of cough syrup and a Stilnox and closed her eyes.

She spent the night paralysed under the bedclothes, coughing, thirsty, sweaty, convinced that Mr Desmoulins was scaling the wall of her house and was trying to open the metal shutters on her window, making horrible grinding noises.

21 October 2009
For the attention of the Deputy Mayor for the
environment

Mr Deputy Mayor,

I read with great satisfaction the piece in the city council's
magazine issue devoted to green spaces in the city. And I
am delighted to live in a town that can boast a four-
flower 'City in Bloom' rating.

I am glad, too, to read your comments in the article
regarding 'planting and landscape heritage' and
'sustainable development'. The use of chemicals is
banned on the city's plants, and city gardeners are
working with organic fertilisers – I myself have been a
natural compost enthusiast for over thirty years. As for
the numbers, they speak for themselves: 40 hectares of
green space, 9,000 trees, 15 kilometres of hedgerows,
372 planters, 250,000 tulip, daffodil and hyacinth
bulbs – you'd think you were reading a garden centre's
promotional leaflet.

I can only encourage you in the development of the

arboretum at Bois de L'Étoile; it seems to be a veritable tree museum, one that I have not yet had the time to visit.

But allow me to enquire after the contrasts of our beautiful city: why cheer up the approach to a train station with abundantly planted containers when a few metres away, buses leave their engines idling while parked along the path, where users don't even have a bus shelter to protect themselves from the elements and breathing in pollutants? And what about that awful old bridge, black with dirt, which spans the main street of the town, causing terrible noise pollution for passers-by and the neighbourhood? None of your delicate little window boxes would last a day attached to the safety barriers against which a cyclist was crushed by a truck some time ago, if memory serves.

Walking under the bridge is my greatest fear. The pavements are ridiculous; it feels like the cars are grazing against you as they pass. The roar of a TGV passing overhead terrifies me, and I'm not the only one. It makes babies and children jump in their buggies. I've nicknamed it 'the devil's mouth'!

This bridge is a wart on our beautiful town. Perhaps the traffic patterns should be reviewed in the area. Perhaps a plan could be developed to vent the sides of the pedestrian passageways in order to shield them from the cars and pollution?

I know you to be a sensitive and generous man; you are a kind man, and it shows. That is why I allowed myself to write you this letter, as you no doubt have some influence with the mayor, and have your views heard, towards maintaining a pleasant environment, and an ecologically balanced urban space for all.

Respectfully yours, and with continued encouragement for your work,

Elsa Préau
(Retired)

39

The green tartan shopping trolley jangled across the tarmac car park. Mrs Préau straightened the scarf under her chin. With apprehensive steps, she entered the Intermarché. There was nothing fun about it. The cashiers had been depressed since their uniform jackets had been replaced with less flattering charcoal-grey blouses. The selection of organic fruits and vegetables was down to the bare minimum, the prices shown corresponded only sometimes to those paid at the till and some of the frozen goods bore a thin layer of frost on the packaging (a sign of earlier thawing). It was advisable to avoid the butcher's counter, where on a Monday some of the pieces of meat took on an aftertaste of cleaning products. But Mrs Préau was a woman of habit, and she had a loyalty card. She enjoyed the brief but warm exchange with the employees whom she began to recognise and whom she passed in the street from time to time. That the range of products and their location never varied an iota suited her down to the ground. She was not tempted by novelty and her wallet was never the worse for wear. Her only trouble was difficulty accessing the red onions (placed in a display at floor-level) and the organic wholegrain biscuits arranged on the top shelf of diet products. Fortunately, there was always a charming gentleman to reach them for her.

Ten days had passed since Martin forced his mother into confinement. The routine of doing her shopping was getting her back on track: dosed with royal jelly, ginseng and magnesium, Mrs Préau pushed her trolley with the resolute air of a future World Championship medallist in swimming. Despite her convalescent pallor and slightly glassy eyes, she had regained her poise, a small woman with a firm chin and a surprisingly straight back for her age. Under her wool coat, she wore a grey scarf around her neck. She put a bag of flour, butter, chocolate, milk and eggs in the bottom of her trolley with a graceful gesture, like a dancer performing an arabesque. If it weren't for a slight raise of her eyelids and the sporadic contractions of her mouth, there would be nothing to suggest that she was preparing to wage a battle against all odds, taking no heed of the indifference of the country's social services. There was nothing to suggest that the whispers of a child accompanied her every step.

Save me, Granny Elsa, save me.

40

Before going to the police, Mrs Préau went to her hair-dresser, an unpretentious salon on Rue Jean Jaurès, close to the chemist. She wanted to make a good impression. Under the purple neon, four sinks, four mirrors and two hairdryers dedicated to permanents made the slow trade still more modest. Yet Jessica, the owner, had painted the walls the same colour as the neon, which pleased the old lady. Mrs Préau had once had raven-black, smooth and silky hair with glints of red or blue depending on her mood. In 1981, she had decided on a bob with a short fringe and a bare neck. 'You look like Joan of Arc,' mocked her son, while Bastien later compared his grand-mother's hair to his Playmobil figurines. Over time, her hair had become coarse, turning the colour of stone. A special treatment for grey hair would revive it and, with two strokes of the scissors, the hairdresser brought her fringe back up to four centimetres.

'Can you imagine? "Gone for cigarettes" is what he told the police. But by the time the neighbour phoned the police, more than two hours had passed. And it took them forty-five minutes to find him! It's just so miserable. Leaving a baby of fifteen months at home alone ... They should be made to pass a test, fathers like that. If you don't have your "parent's licence", you have no right to have kids! Tilt your head there, Mrs Préau. How is the water temperature?'

It was lovely to have her hair washed by Catherine, her favourite hairdresser. Catherine had gentle little gestures and didn't speak to the customers much except when she was in a snit about something. Mrs Préau liked her idea of a parenting licence. She would give some thought to writing a new letter to that effect to the Prime Minister, François Fillon. But her neck was resting on the edge of the basin, which was tormenting her, so she asked Catherine to hurry in applying a treatment. With her skull swaddled in a towel like a Hollywood starlet just out of her bath, she sat in a chair next to the bay window to watch the world go by as the rain beat down.

I'm cold, Granny Elsa.

The little boy spoke to her more and more often. He communicated with her especially in the kitchen, where

Mrs Préau regularly heard small knocks from inside the cabinets. There was undoubtedly a meaning behind it, unless it was just the wood settling. He was there, in Evan's salon, lying against her, putting invisible kisses on her cheeks.

'Do you have something to read while I wait?'

Mrs Préau took the magazine she was offered, put on her glasses and began reading *Hello!* She was up to the 'Hot/Not' list when a shrill whistle in her left ear made her look up. Taking off her glasses, Mrs Préau looked around to see what could have caused such a noise. Leaning to her side, she saw a woman sitting with her back to her a few metres away. The owner was cutting her hair.

Mrs Préau recognised the face reflected in the mirror.

Mrs Desmoulins went to the same salon!

This changed everything.

Cautiously, the old lady stood up. She had no desire to meet this woman's gaze. The only thing she wanted was to crush her fingers bone by bone with the hammer in her purse until she admitted that she was keeping her eldest son locked up. But Mrs Préau was a realist. Such behaviour would be out of place in a hair salon. She had to try a different approach. Tempt fate by going to the police. The Desmoulins weren't that powerful. At least she hoped not.

'The treatment didn't work, then? First thing's first: a vinegar rinse.'

Snatches of their conversation reached her between the running taps and the din of a hairdryer. It seemed to be about nits in Kévin's hair.

'Have you been to see the chemist next door? Because she has some good products.'

The old lady winced. Kévin had lice? She waited until Mrs Desmoulins had left the salon to ask the hairdressers a few questions. As far as they knew, yes, there were two children in the Desmoulins family. The little ones came to the salon.

'They don't have the hair for head lice, the Desmoulins kids. Normally, you'll get everything with the first shampoo on hair like theirs. My son, though – the lice just thread themselves onto his curls like beads. That'll be thirty-two euro, Mrs Préau. Will I give you a bottle of the whitener as well?'

'That won't be necessary, thank you.'

The old lady slipped four euro into a pink neon piggy on the counter and added: 'Can I ask you something? Have you been getting regular phone calls about installing windows in the last month or two?'

The question seemed to surprise the hairdressers. When they shook their heads, Mrs Préau nodded.

'That's what I thought.'

Then she added with irony, 'For your information,

Mr Desmoulins can get you good prices on double-glazing.'

Protected by her umbrella, she left the salon certain that the stone boy had passed the lice on to his younger brother and that she was now being harassed. It was time to go to the police.

Notes: Saturday 24 October

Lovely police officer. Assures me that the commissioner and the police chief look at the desk sergeant's logbook every day, and an alleged abuse case would be quickly taken in hand.

Saw a poster on the wall at the police station of an outstretched hand, with leaflets about ongoing, dedicated support to victims. There's a woman at the police station who has been offering to listen to and provide support for victims every day from 9 to 5 for a year now. I am relieved to see that such initiatives exist in France. The police officer, who is originally from Guadeloupe, told me that the logbook frequently cites acts of violence against women. They only rarely lead to complaints. Women do not know their rights and are dying of fear. Especially young African women.

On my return, I met Ms Blanche on Rue des Lilas. She was carrying a plastic bag on her head to protect herself from the rain. A soggy baguette and a few newspapers were sticking out of the bag. We exchanged a few words. I warned her against the cats, but she already knew about the microchips. She let me know that a mast to improve mobile phone reception had been installed recently 150 metres from my house, just opposite the railway station on the Villemomble side. It seems that these antennas emit microwaves, which have disastrous effects on your health. Some hypersensitive people could develop serious diseases. She told me about a supplement to Geo magazine that investigated cutting-edge technology. The Israeli military has a sensitive, super-lightweight motion sensor apparatus that sends information to a remote control unit. Also, an ultra-high-frequency device that can see through walls.

It's very worrying.

We are never sheltered from view.

And yet, they've never hidden so much from us.

My headaches have worsened since this strange flu. Are they caused by micro-radiation?

Getting rid of the cats has become a priority.

41

By Sunday morning, Martin had still not brought the
camera his mother needed. Mrs Préau had to walk to the
Monoprix to get one for herself.

'It won't read it.'

The old lady started as she adjusted her beret.

'I beg your pardon?'

The cashier repeated it again, passing the item in front
of the scanner. The name Tiphaine was pinned on her
blouse.

'Nothing doing,' she repeated. 'Where did you find it?'

It had to happen with this particular item. Mrs Préau
sighed.

'At the cheese display,' she said. 'Why?'

Some cashiers could be so stupid. She would never be

able to do it. How could you ask such a question about a disposable camera? The bottle of green apple liqueur, the roll of aluminium foil and a packet of weed killer passed the laser beam test without incident.

Sing something for me, Granny Elsa.

On the way back, she gave Bastien her hand and hummed a song about a chestnut tree, followed by one about a short man who had broken his nose.

At noon, she prepared a special menu for the cats seasoned with Roundup herbicide, a veritable killing machine.

At one o'clock, she started collecting the little cadavers in the garden.

There would be more. Some of them only came at nightfall.

Burying them was out of the question. The microchips should be disabled, and covering them with soil wouldn't be enough for that. Mrs Préau had been doing research at the library, perusing the work of one Ralph State, assistant scientist at the University of Luxembourg, who knew a lot about the subject. These microchips or 'passive transponders', the size of a grain of rice, had a coil that could be activated remotely and respond in echo to a radio wave according to a predetermined code. Equipped with a cellular antenna receiver/transmitter, they could activate their memory at any time, energy being generated by the identification marker.

Information was exchanged instantaneously. The applications of these chips were many; in certain cases, they had been implanted in humans, such as royal heirs, with the aim of preventing kidnappings. But Mrs Préau was not fooled by the primary purpose of these vehicles of destruction.

There was indeed a way to disable them. If a chip were subjected to a brief pulse from an intense magnetic field, the stress generated by induction would be sufficient to destroy its circuits, like any other electronic device.

But Mrs Préau had no machine to create a magnetic field. She did, however, have a washing machine. The 90-degree white cotton cycle would be more than enough to deactivate even the most resistant components.

42

At three o'clock, she was at her post, camera in hand. It was a rudimentary thing: you put your eye at one opening and pressed a button. Mrs Préau was nervous. Again that night she hadn't slept because of the rain pounding on the roof and the infernal racket of mice in the attic, so she didn't get to sleep until dawn. She had drunk too much tea to fight off drowsiness, and when she stretched her hands out in front of her, her fingers trembled. To ease the palpitations, after her Sunday vegetable soup and a few figs, she served herself a generous *digestif*, which warmed up her ears. The neighbours' soggy garden looked like a battlefield. Would her little soldier have the courage to show himself?

Laurie and Kévin were the first out of the house,

wrapped up in fur-lined parkas. Laurie picked up a ball and threw it smack in her brother's face, producing the first scream. Kévin ran after his sister, seeking revenge, but she surprised him, suddenly pushing him away, hard. He fell on his bottom and howled, his trousers covered in mud. The cruel game continued for ten minutes, and their indifferent parents stayed inside the house. Finally, Mr Desmoulins showed his nasty face on the porch. Lighting a cigarette, he told Kévin to go back inside. Whining, covered with dirt, the child trudged towards his father, who slapped him on the back of the head to hurry him back indoors. Visibly satisfied, Laurie had taken over the swing and lifted her legs up high to get the most out of the upswing, giving a nod to her dad. Mrs Préau sighed. She would have loved to have straightened out the brat. But, after all, it was up to Kévin to learn how to fight back, to rebel against his sister's authoritarianism. In time, he would grow up and eventually smack her back.

Suddenly, the boy appeared behind Mr Desmoulins. Almost a shadow, a ghostly apparition. He stood stooped, his face bent over his dirty trainers, and he was swimming in his jacket. A red cap that was too narrow had been pushed onto his head, and it stood up, cone-shaped, à la Jacques Cousteau. Mrs Préau put down the binoculars and snatched up the camera. The child was partly hidden by his father. He had to come forward for her to take his picture. But he did not move. It looked like he was waiting for something. The sound of Mrs Préau's piano? After what seemed like an infinitely long time, the boy took a few steps forward, dragging his feet. He was now alone in the viewfinder. The old lady moved the forefinger of her right hand and released the shutter. That's when something incredible happened. The child looked up abruptly, staring towards Mrs Préau's window, and made a sound. The most terrifying sound the retired teacher had ever heard. Like a pig having its throat cut, shrill and guttural. Appalled, Mrs Préau staggered, almost losing her balance. She caught onto the headboard and put a hand to her heart. It only took her a few seconds to regain her composure, but when she returned to the window, the father had thrown down his cigarette and was dragging the stone boy along the ground by the collar of his jacket. The boy was writhing, struggling fiercely to free himself from being strangled by his clothing. From the swing, Laurie witnessed the scene impassively. Mrs Préau had a world of trouble to take a picture, she was trembling so much. The boy's back jolted as it made contact with the steps leading up to the front door, and then the father grabbed the child and threw him inside the house, swearing.

There wasn't another noise to be heard in the Desmoulins' garden.

Then, little by little, Laurie signalled her presence with

the creak of the swing. There she was, oblivious to what had happened.

Mrs Préau sat on the bed. She held out a hand to the drawer of her nightstand and pulled out a box of pills and tried to swallow one. But her hand missed her mouth and the medicine fell to the floor. The old lady got down on all fours to find it, then collapsed, sobbing.

Save me, Granny Elsa. They'll kill me!

43

'What is going on?'

'What do you mean, what's going on?'

'You told me to come as soon as possible, that it was a matter of life or death.'

'Don't you want to sit down?'

Martin hadn't removed his coat. He paced the hall, furious at having been worried about his mother.

'No, I do not want to sit down! I want to know what's going on here! First, I want to know why I can never reach you on the phone. Don't tell me you've unplugged it again . . .'

Mrs Préau shrugged.

'I leave it off the hook on the weekend as a precaution.

I'm tired of being disturbed by the neighbour. I made tea, you want some?'

'The neighbour? What neighbour?'

The old lady went to the kitchen, turning her back on Martin.

'He works for Lapeyre. Oh, I know what they want! Under the pretext of selling me double-glazing, they try to get me to fall into their trap. But I wasn't born yesterday. Milk and sugar?'

Martin's mobile vibrated in his pocket. He sighed before answering. The conversation was short.

'No, she's fine . . . I don't know . . . I said I don't know! I'll call you back . . . no. I'll be there in twenty minutes. Love you too.'

A moment later, he was watching his mother drink her tea in the lounge, refusing to drink even a glass of water. Fairly annoyed, he put his Nokia on the table-cloth.

'I promise you, everything is fine, Martin.'

'No, it is not fine. You cannot call me for help, and a quarter of an hour later behave as if nothing happened. What happened at about four o'clock today? You had a psychotic episode, is that it?'

Hesitating, Mrs Préau stroked her teacup with her fingertips. She regretted having called her son before waiting for the half a Stilnox to be absorbed.

'Look, I didn't want to tell you about it before because

I didn't want to worry you. But terrible things are hap-pening in the house across the street, Martin.'

The man clapped his hands over his face.

'Oh, that's all I need.'

'But it's the truth. I've been watching them for months. There's a child who—'

'Shut up, Mum. That's enough!'

'Don't you want to hear what I have to say? Why would I have called you for help? Or rather, for whom? There's a little fellow who looks exactly like Bastien, who—'

'Are you not taking it any more?' he barked. 'Tell me the truth.'

Mrs Préau leaned back in her chair. She was silent, embarrassed.

'Audrette thinks you have stopped taking your medi-cation. Is that true?'

'My medication has nothing to do with it, Martin. It turns out that—'

A fist slammed down on the table.

'Well, shit!'

Martin leapt up and started pacing with his head down, turning in circles, not knowing what to do with his hands, muttering about his mother, the crazy loon who was ruining his life and would keep on ruining it until the day she dropped. He thought he was the only one to blame because he hadn't had the courage to accept that she was completely crazy, refusing to put her in care because it seemed to him that, broadly speaking, she was independent; she ate well, behaved well enough and basically kept her nose clean. Despite the traumas suffered in recent years, she had responded pretty well so far and seemed to be on the mend, but now it had started again: she was seeing little people everywhere.

'No. Never in my life,' Mrs Préau corrected, savouring her green tea. 'I've never had such visions. You're talking rubbish.'

'And when you ask me for news of Bastien every time we see each other or talk on the phone, aren't you, perhaps, being delusional?'

'It's normal for me to worry about my grandson.'

'But Mum, Bastien is dead!'

Martin's fist struck the table for a second time. His face contorted with rage; he looked like one of those union workers ready to do anything to keep up the strike. Mrs Préau remained unmoved.

'I do not believe that the photographs the judge showed me back then were actually of Bastien.'

Exasperated, Martin left the room.

'Where are you going?'

He left without kissing his mother. The sound of his car engine reverberated to the end of the street.

Mrs Préau didn't like it when they argued. She knew exactly which devil had sowed discord between them.

Now, she knew to expect the worst. Probably injections – she loathed injections. Who knew if Martin would make good on his threat and put his mother in an old people's home; Audrette had her eye on the house, no doubt. She had always known how to manipulate her son, to the point of making him blind to his own actions. She would have to handle him more carefully. Mrs Préau would write a letter of apology to her beloved son to enrage the bitch. Changing the locks on her house to which Martin had the keys was also a priority. She had to stay here by hook or by crook until the stone boy was saved.

Something vibrated on the table, and she jumped. Her son had forgotten his mobile phone.

The bright screen displayed Audrette's name in capital letters. Mrs Préau watched the thing until it stopped flashing. Then, returning from the kitchen with a dustpan and brush, she cautiously slid it into the dustpan and went down to the basement to put on a wash.

Monday 26 October 2009

Martin,

I'm sorry to have upset you so yesterday. It was not my intention. I received a severe blow myself that afternoon by witnessing a terrible scene in my neighbours' garden — as I tried to tell you, they hit one of their sons. You know how sensitive a subject violence against children is for me. What you took for a delusion is unfortunately only the truth. Dr Mamnoue has been aware of it for several weeks. I have also alerted social services, and I made an official statement to the police on Friday. I needed to share this with you, that's all. I'm so sorry that things turned out so badly.

As for the camera that you forgot to bring me, I managed in the end. I bought one that is doing the trick for the moment. And I reconnected the phone this morning. About the shutters — I prefer to wait until they have dismantled the crane before opening them again. But I will do it, don't worry. I have a holy horror of dust mites!

I have to go. I have just received a call from a Ms Tremblay from the police who wants to meet with me about my statement.

Again, forgive me for causing you all this upset.

I think this wretched flu has made me very weak and no doubt affected me psychologically over recent days, but I'll get through it.

We live in difficult times, but we will win out in the end, you'll see.

Affectionately,

Mum

PS: Did you know that a relay antenna to improve mobile phone reception has been erected in front of my house on the other side of the station? (You can see it from the first-floor bathroom.) Isn't it dangerous for my health?

44

She was courteously received. Ms Tremblay was about forty years old and looked like a typical single mother. She had short hair, a beige polo-neck jumper, an olive complexion; a woman in a hurry who did a slapdash job of putting on her make-up without taking care of her skin. At the back of her office was a window that overlooked the nearby gym. The social worker, for this was her title, was interested in domestic violence, family disputes and at-risk minors. Her role of listening to and supporting victims went as far as making care orders and organising placements. Every day, she consulted police reports filed the day before and took note of any cases that fell within her jurisdiction.

'This morning I read an electronic copy of the report you filed on Friday. Considering the content, I decided to call you immediately. Would you like a coffee? I've just made one for myself.'

A ceramic mug with a penguin on it landed in her hands.

'If you want sugar . . . '

She pushed a cup filled with wrapped sugar cubes towards Mrs Préau, which she politely refused. The woman in the beige jumper asked essentially the same questions as Ms Polin, but more delicately. She thought the old lady brave to take this step, and didn't question her about her age.

'Often, people are surprised when they first learn that their neighbour is being beaten by her husband all day long. They admit that seeing her leave the house with black eyes or an arm in a cast threw up a few question marks, but nothing more. Is your coffee OK?'

This Ms Tremblay was friendly. Her sense of irony and her concern pleased Mrs Préau, and they both bought the same Nescafé.

'It's Green Blend with antioxidants, isn't it?' enquired the old lady.

'I like it a lot. It has a slightly fruity taste.'

'Yes, it's very mild.' Mrs Préau unbuttoned her coat.

'Still, don't be fooled. It's only thirty-five per cent green coffee. The rest is roasted.'

'Yes, and the antioxidant thing is mostly marketing. At .4 grams per cup of coffee, it would take hundreds of litres a day to feel the beneficial effects on the body.'

'Yes. You'd be better off snacking on dark chocolate.'

'Oh, yes!'

Ever careful, Mrs Préau still held her handbag against her, its false base concealing a hammer; she wasn't to be parted from it. That said, she felt almost at ease, except for one detail: the office door was left ajar. Muffled voices coming from the hallway of the police station were distracting the old lady. She leaned towards the woman, and in a whisper confided in her about the failure of her approach to social services. Ms Tremblay replied in the same tone.

'Contacting social services was the first step to be taken. And it saves us time. They don't necessarily take the same approach to their file, although our findings generally overlap. I'll contact them for more information.'

Mrs Préau got the disposable camera wrapped in a plastic bag out of her handbag.

'I took some pictures yesterday. I hope they are not too blurry, I haven't had much practice. What I saw happen in the garden was so violent ...'

'Yes, these are not generally the kind of photos neighbours take; they're usually naked poolside shots. Much more pleasant.'

'I'll get them developed. Perhaps ...' Mrs Préau crossed her arms.

'Do. But I don't think that at this stage a photo of the child is necessary. And, I am not in a position to take this kind of thing into account. My job is to relay information. But these photos could be valuable for the CPIO. I'll make some calls and get back to you shortly. Would you by any chance be related to Dr Préau?'

The old lady was taken aback by the question.

'Yes, why?' she stammered, putting the camera back in her handbag.

'I was a patient of his a few years ago. He's a very good doctor. He is still practising?'

'Yes, he is. His office is in Pavillons-sous-Bois.'

Ms Tremblay's cheeks took on a pretty pink colour. The old lady knew then which of her son's talents in particular the woman was alluding to, and immediately relaxed.

This could strengthen her credibility in the file.

This is perhaps why she was offered a coffee.

Mrs Préau had given birth to a beautiful boy. Her great tragedy. The fairer sex soon stole him away from her, and the affectionate kisses of a little boy dried as quickly as he had grown. Now past forty, he looked like that American actor who wielded a whip and fought the Nazis whom she had seen on the big screen at the Grand Rex in Paris. It had been one of the last times that, as a teenager, Martin had begged his mother to go with him to the cinema. After that, he went with his girlfriends.

'If you see him, will you give him my best? Valérie Tremblay.'

The two women shook hands. Leaving the social worker's office, Mrs Préau passed a policeman in his fifties who had a debonair look about him. He bowed graciously. Mrs Préau quickened her pace. Something about the man rubbed her up the wrong way, like when you are reminded of a bitter memory. She was eager to get her ID card, which she had left at reception, to get out of the police station, and to find a photo lab and an open locksmith – which wasn't likely on a Monday when shops tended to be closed.

45

More than a hundred mousetraps had been set at various spaces around the house; not a single critter ventured near one. Either it was a question of a breed of superior intelligence (developed in a laboratory by the FBI) or Mrs Préau was suffering from tinnitus: it hissed and whistled whenever silence fell around her. These bothersome nocturnal noises that faded at dawn could be caused by damage to the eardrum and might explain the increased frequency of her headaches. The old lady preferred not to make a call on it, even though the latter was the more likely hypothesis. All these years listening to children screaming in the playground had damaged her hearing. The same symptoms had occurred ten years ago and this damned flu had not helped her ENT health.

'Me, I've never had the flu. I'm against it.'

On Tuesday morning, Mr Apeldoorn was grouchy. The flu was decimating his patients and Mrs Préau was one of the few survivors who could manage to lift weights in his office.

'I'm deathly afraid of athlete's foot. It's the greatest threat to physiotherapists. Come on, a little effort from the miraculous risen of H1N1. Lift that for me.'

'It's heavy, Mr Apeldoorn.'

'There's no room for such nonsense between us. And next we have to fatten you up a bit, eh? You've lost muscle and fat. This isn't the swimsuit season plan any more.'

Mrs Préau smiled. But a quarter of an hour later, she refused electro-stimulation.

'What do you mean, "no"?'

'Mr Apeldoorn, I'm not sure that this electrical current flowing through my body is beneficial.'

'You're afraid of turning into a radio receiver?' joked the physio while unhooking pulleys from saddlebags full of lead balls.

'You're not far from the truth, Mr Apeldoorn. Here's a tip: you should remove the fillings from your teeth, as a preventive measure.'

'Bah! Where did you get that idea?'

'It's because of waves and radiation. I don't want to turn into a neutron bomb. I prefer to stick to the gymnastics.'

She ended her session with Mr Apeldoorn looking puzzled, and then went on to the photo lab and the lock-smith. The photos would be developed in under twenty-four hours and the two locks (the front door and the kitchen door into the garden) were scheduled to be changed on Thursday at two o'clock. In the meantime, the old lady would take care to jam the backs of dining-room chairs under the door handles.

They could come and get her: she was ready and waiting with her hammer.

46

Laurie grabbed a spoon and tucked in to the raspberry tart.
The little musician had pleased her teacher for the second
time and was eating the home-made dessert greedily. Mrs
Préau scrutinised the child's face, looking into her clear
blue eyes for a sign of a rift, a call for help, but found
nothing but cheekiness and greed. The old lady sighed.
She had to take a more aggressive strategy. A word from
the little sister could save her brother. But is that what she
wanted? Wasn't she under the influence of the father, too?
How many children hushed up violence against other
family members for fear of becoming the target?

'It's gourmet week at school,' the girl blurted. 'The
teacher said we'd have crêpes on Thursday.'

'Have you ever flipped crêpes in a frying pan?'

'No.'

'If you like, next week, I'll make the batter, and after your lesson, you can put on an apron and we'll make them for your whole family.'

'OK. But we'll have to be fast because Mum doesn't want me to stay too long at your house.' Laurie took the glass of water and drank down half of it.

Mrs Préau then started in on the most delicate part of the conversation.

'Have you heard of parents who spank their children, Laurie?'

The child's face darkened. She didn't answer.

'In the past, parents sometimes beat their children. But now, society has changed. We protect girls and boys better. You know that parents no longer have the right to spank children, and teachers don't either?'

'Teachers give punishments, that's all.'

'Well, it's the same for parents. They have to respect their children's bodies, because they don't belong to them. What is the role of parents, Laurie?'

Laurie squirmed in her chair, drawing circles on the oilcloth with the back of the spoon.

'I don't know.'

'You don't know?'

'My mum takes care of the house and she picks us up at school. She does the cooking, too. And in the evening, she reads to me.'

Mrs Préau crossed her arms, her voice softening.

'You're lucky, Laurie, to have a nice mum who reads books to you. Some children aren't so lucky. Some children have mean parents.'

'My parents aren't mean. It's just that Dad gets angry sometimes.'

'Your dad, does he get angry with your little brother sometimes?'

Laurie tucked her chin into her chest and shrugged.

'My dad sometimes spanks us,' she said sheepishly.

Her teacher felt like she had made a breakthrough. She pushed ahead.

'If your dad were hurting your brother, would you speak to someone? To your teacher?'

The child pushed away the plate and spoon, refusing to answer. She wanted to go. Mrs Préau helped her put on her coat and while she tied the scarf around her neck, she whispered in her ear: 'I'll tell you a secret, Laurie. There's a phone number that only children can call. A number with only three digits. It's a magic number. You can dial it from any phone.'

'119?'

'Yes. If some day you saw an adult hurt a child or hurt you, then you should call the magic number and tell the person who answers.'

The little girl was intrigued.

'Who answers, then?'

'A man or a woman, someone who listens to and pro-
tects children. But we mustn't talk about it to anyone. It's
very important. Not even your mother. It's a secret.'

Laurie went out onto the front porch, dubious.

'How come you know it, then, the magic number?'

Mrs Préau smiled mischievously.

'Because I was a teacher at your school. And all the
nice teachers know 119.' Laurie nodded, satisfied, before
trotting down the steps. Children's logic was Mrs Préau's
special subject.

After she escorted her student home, Mrs Préau
received a phone call from her son. He was looking for
his Nokia. She swore that he had left her house with it
on Sunday night, and was worried about whether he had
received her letter.

'We'll talk about it on Thursday. I'll come round at
around noon.'

Martin hung up without wishing her a good day, as he
had always done, even when he was furious at her.

Mrs Préau worried herself sick from then on.

47

'Do you understand, Elsa?'

'Yes, perfectly, Claude.'

'It's a matter of trust between the two of you.'

'Absolutely.'

'So how do you see Martin? As a doctor, or as a son?'

Mrs Préau shrugged and sighed.

'What do you want? He is his father's son.'

'His *father's* son. Martin has no mother, then?'

The old lady pouted, dubious, and scratched her chin. The discussion made her uncomfortable. Since the beginning of the session, they had only spoken about Martin.

'That's not what I mean. Martin is my son, of course, but he mostly takes after his father: same job, same desire to succeed, same size, and they're both ladies' men . . . Both of them abandoned me at a point in my life where—'

'You think that Martin abandoned you?'

Mrs Préau bit the inside of her cheek. It was difficult to answer that without saying 'yes'.

'Do you think that a man is selfish for deciding to devote himself to his career, to his work, rather than staying with his mother?'

'When in excess, yes, in a way,' she said in a thin voice.

'And when your son spends three nights at your bedside without returning home, he's only doing his duty as a doctor?'

Mrs Préau stiffened in the armchair. She looked at the hands of the man sitting in front of her. The right held a Montblanc ballpoint pen, the other turned down the left corner of the page in front of him. She had never seen him write during their sessions, and yet he thought it necessary to take notes today.

Dr Mamnoue had spoken with Martin on the phone.

Otherwise, how could he know about the three nights at her bedside?

Martin had certainly alerted him to the fragile mental state of his patient.

Unbeknownst to her, Dr Mamnoue was going through an assessment to measure how potentially dangerous Mrs Préau might be. This was not the time to talk to her about tinnitus. He immediately equated her hearing troubles with a hallucinatory delirium and wondered if she had stopped taking her medication.

'Didn't he show you a lot of love in the past?'

'I don't want to talk about it.'

'You don't want to talk about what, Elsa, the past or the love that Martin has for you?'

A grey veil. Mrs Préau's past had little more to it than a greying lace curtain hanging in a window, quivering in the breeze. She saw the dancing shadows of her mother, father, husband and Bastien, each wearing the mask of silence.

They were all so far away.

There was no one to hold her hand now.

To rest their head against her heart. To kiss her.

Mrs Préau, like many older people, suffered from no longer being touched. Falling ill or complaining of a bad back were their only recourse. It was only because of a bad flu that Martin rested his palm on his mother's forehead; Mr Apeldoorn only massaged her back with his burning hands on prescription.

Dr Mamnoue remained silent. Mrs Préau smiled.

'Bastien used to kiss me often. I used to have his little arms around my neck like a necklace. At the age of three, he was so loving, telling me, "Granny Elsa, I love you" all day long. His skin was so soft and warm, the scent of his hair so delicious ... Sometimes he would stay overnight at my house. His little slippers, toothbrush and pyjamas were all there. When he left with his parents, I slept in his sheets to breathe his scent again ... '

'You probably did the same thing with Martin when he was a child.'

'Yes. Well, I think so. That was different. He was in the house every day. And I worked a lot at the time, too. I think I missed out on quite a few things with Martin. When his father left, he had a growth spurt. In six months, he went up two trouser sizes.'

Mrs Préau apologised, took a handkerchief from her bag and blew her nose loudly. The sound produced was childlike.

'For someone who's convalescing, you're in good shape,' he remarked. 'You bounced back from this terrible virus remarkably well.'

'Honestly, Claude, I don't think I did have swine flu – and if I did, this big vaccination campaign must be nothing more than a plot by the French government to give a lot of money to pharmaceutical companies. What do you think? Did I actually have the flu, or am I totally paranoid?'

Dr Mamnoue chuckled. Recapping his pen, he said in an affectionate tone, 'You are what you are, Elsa. But best that you not get it again.'

He stood up and held out a hand to the old lady to help leave her chair.

'Martin will call you at the end of the week. He's

considering the best way to support you as a doctor and as a son. But you should know that I advised him to put you in the hands of a colleague: Dr Leclerc. He's an excellent GP.'

'Really?'

Dr Mamnoue gave his patient a friendly pat on the shoulder, but she had already lost out to panic, her pupils dilated.

'It is high time, Elsa. For both of us.'

Notes: Thursday 29 October

Woken by the noise of the dustbin men at six o'clock. I spent the night on the couch in the living room next to the radio switched on the lowest volume. I can't stand hearing these noises in my head. Sometimes I feel like the keys on the piano are jangling intermittently. I also always hear knocking in the kitchen cupboards.

The quality of the photos is mediocre. They're too dark. I asked the photographer to enlarge the one that I took of the child so that we could see his face, but the photographer explained to me that shooting from this distance, with low daylight, the graininess can't be helped. As for the other photos, the ones where he's being dragged along the ground by his father, they're blurry.

Everything has to be redone. These disposable cameras live up to their name.

Waited for Martin until half past twelve. In the end, he won't be coming today. Too much work, so he says. Postponed his visit to Saturday. He'll come at the same time as the nurse. My son has, it would seem, decided to give me Risperdal injections.

I do not want to turn into a zombie two days per week.

Fortunately, the locksmith has just finished his work. Isabelle did the cleaning quickly this morning. She's not happy because I put padlocks on the shutters. I know she opened them to air the place when my back was turned! I held back from telling her that her key wouldn't work in the door any more. I don't want her to tell Martin about it. I just have to keep a lookout through the window in the morning to let her in when she arrives.

The cats' bowl has been full for two days. At least I got rid of the plague.

Received a call at three from Ms Tremblay, very annoyed. Said nothing to be done in the current state of things. There is no trace of a third child in the Desmoulins family on either the father's or the mother's side. She even did research in the town where they lived previously in the suburbs of Auxerre, where Mrs Desmoulins' family lives. No other child has been enrolled in school there under the name of Desmoulins. I suggested that she dig deeper, and consider the possibility of an adopted or stolen child. Ms Tremblay is doubtful. In the first case, the child would appear in the family record. The latter case seems far-fetched to her. I think *she lacks imagination for a social worker assigned to a council estate police station. Yet she must be accustomed to seeing people who are underdeveloped, emotionally disturbed sadists and perverts capable of anything, including stealing kids to make them their sex slaves. However, I clearly managed to convince her, because she asked me to bring the picture of the stone boy in as soon as I get the enlargement on Friday. She plans to pass it to a colleague – an ex child protection officer – to launch a possible investigation into a disappearance. But she added: 'I don't hold out much hope.'*

She's right.

A photo of an unknown child in my neighbours' garden is not proof in itself: it may very well be a friend of Laurie's or Kévin's.

Back to square one. I would drop off the jar of red pebbles and the burst ball filled with soil, but I'm afraid they'd think I was crazy. However, if they did a DNA test on the dried blood like they did on these television shows, they would know that I was right.

It's all a waste of time.

It's been four days since I took the pictures.

And Bastien isn't appearing to me any more.

I can't wait any longer.

I have to act.

I'll head over to the Intermarché to buy cider and fresh eggs.

48

Mrs Préau's baking filled the house with the scent of vanilla. Isabelle cleaned all morning, dreaming of the delicious madeleines that the old lady dipped in dark chocolate before leaving them to dry on a baking sheet.

'They're bad for you,' she teased when Isabelle came a little too close to the kitchen table where an apple tart was cooling.

The housekeeper left, slamming the door as usual – that woman had never known how to use a door handle. Mrs Préau then prepared the bottle of cider: using a syringe, she pricked through the cap, and injected the equivalent of five Stilnox that she had ground into a powder and dissolved in a teaspoon of water before chilling the drink. Even if the Desmoulins' father didn't have a sweet tooth, he wouldn't refuse a little glass of country cider, beer lover that he was.

The old lady then went out to the post office with a tied-up package that she had prepared the night before. There, they wanted to force her to invest in a cardboard box at an exorbitant price, which they justified by the fact that the package could then be identified by a unique barcode, which reduced the risk of loss and allowed it to be tracked on its journey. Mrs Préau refused to let them put a barcode on her package.

'Don't you want to tattoo a number on my arm while you're at it?' she growled at the customer service agent sitting behind the counter, a North African thirty-something with sloping shoulders.

She bought and stuck on the requisite number of stamps to send an ordinary item and handed it over to the puzzled agent. The package would take a few extra days to arrive, but at least no one could intercept it and destroy its contents.

At one, she stretched out on her bed, covering her legs with a blanket. The alarm went off at three. With a slight headache, Mrs Préau came down to loosen the madeleines one by one. She arranged them on a white porcelain cake stand and turned out the tart, half-sprinkled with cinnamon, onto a silver tray, which Isabelle restored to its original glory each month with a dusting cloth and some silver polish. Then she played Debussy, Chopin, Scott

Joplin and still more Schumann on her piano, trying with each fluid stroke to chase away the hissing and whistling that gushed from both sides of the house.

For fifteen minutes, she stood motionless in her kitchen, facing the window: fringed by purple and golden yellow foliage, the fruit trees were about to lose their leaves; the October sky reddened. In the garden, the railway line rose to the level of the property wall. On the platform, she saw two RER trains pull away with a final groan in opposite directions.

Mrs Préau put on her lined boots, threw a shawl over her shoulders and slipped the hammer behind her back, held firmly by the waistband of her support tights. Then, with the cake stand and bottle of cider in a Monoprix plastic bag and the tray covered with a tea towel under one arm, she left the house, bolting the door. She also closed the gate, and could not help but look up at the crane whose muffled growl meant it was still active at this late hour of the afternoon. She could make out a spy from the County Council lurking in the shadows of the cabin, carefully taking note of her comings and goings.

Mrs Préau smirked.

If they knew what she was about to do, they wouldn't let her calmly cross the road like this; they'd set a SWAT team on her.

49

On the third ring, the gate opened. Mr Desmoulins, in jeans and a green sweatshirt, could not hide his surprise and embarrassment at the old lady arriving uninvited. Mrs Préau, however, was not surprised to see him at home at half five on a Friday; he came home early from work on Fridays. Sometimes, the Kangoo would even be back in the garage by two. Lapeyre employees were entitled to flexible working hours.

'Hello, Mr Desmoulins, I came to bring some cakes for the children's tea-time. I hope they haven't already eaten. They're home-made,' she added, blushing.

The man scratched his neck and head.

'Hello, Mrs Préau. That's very kind of you. But, uh, to what do we owe the honour?'

'I thought it was time that we get better acquainted. After all, we have been neighbours for several months. I brought a bottle of cider too.'

'You shouldn't have gone to all this trouble for us.'

Hesitantly, Mr Desmoulins opened the gate.

'Do excuse the mess, we weren't expecting you ... Blandine!'

Walking across the short, unkempt grass, past the clothes dryer and swing, not turning to look at the weeping birch, watching the approach to the lion's den that was the Desmoulins' house – which they had tried in vain to improve the appearance of by putting flowering window boxes in two of the windows – was already a difficult task in itself, especially as the silver tray began to weigh.

'Wait, let me help you.'

The man grabbed the pink bag and tray and went ahead of Mrs Préau, calling his wife to the rescue.

'Blandine! Our neighbour has come to visit!'

It wasn't long before she made an appearance on the front steps wearing dark blue tracksuit bottoms, taking Kévin by the hand. She was stunned. A rueful smile spread across her scrubbed face.

'Hello, Mrs Préau,' she murmured, holding out a warm hand. 'How nice of you to pay us a visit.'

'She brought cider and cakes,' her husband said, pointing to the things as if to justify himself.

They warned her a second time about the mess that prevailed in the house and to which she shouldn't pay attention: raising two unruly children like Laurie and Kévin required a lot of work; it was difficult to keep the house in order.

Mrs Préau readjusted her shawl, discreetly checking that the hammer at her back hadn't moved.

'I know all about it, don't worry,' said the old lady, trying to be reassuring. 'I myself have raised a son, a monkey, a goat and dozens of one-eyed cats.'

They gave a hollow laugh at what hadn't been a joke and led their surprise guest towards the living room to the left of the entrance. At the back of the room, a low cabinet supported a fabulous television screen almost as wide as the wall. A worn brown sofa darkened the space, which was lit by a rudimentary halogen lamp. Sitting in the middle of the cushions, Laurie was watching a cartoon.

'Kévin and Laurie, say hello to Mrs Préau.'

Kévin held out his cheek, not at all shy. The little girl walked up to her teacher and kissed her perfunctorily on each cheek.

'Come on, Laurie, what's got into you? Aren't you happy to see your piano teacher?'

Laurie nodded.

'Yes.'

This girl wasn't as stupid as she looked. Unlike her

parents, she twigged that the presence of Mrs Préau in the house might be the precursor to a terrible drama.

The old lady stroked her cheek.

'I made chocolate madeleines for you and your little brother. Do you like them?'

This time, the child nodded with more enthusiasm. Appealing to her sense of greed was what worked best with the girl. Mrs Préau had understood that. It was then that she heard the first knock behind her. A muffled sound, almost imperceptible.

Mrs Préau turned her head.

Granny Elsa, I'm here . . .

The voice was low.

The child was dying.

The visitor found herself facing an open-plan kitchen of which the dining area was about ten square metres. The single-storey house wasn't more than a hundred square metres.

'Philippe oversaw the work two years ago when we moved,' Mrs Desmoulins thought to explain while she composed herself. 'We had to change builders three times. People in the construction business aren't reliable . . . '

The kitchen was impeccable, with its massive white-painted wooden doors and pink marble countertops. Obviously, Mr Desmoulins had taken advantage of factory prices at Lapeyre. They invited the neighbour to sit down, took out the plates and dessert forks, put water on to boil for tea, arranged the cake stand and massive silver platter with the tart on the table, and uncorked the cider.

'Blandine, we need glasses,' piped up the husband.

Mrs Desmoulins apologised for her forgetfulness and rose to get them in the kitchen. Kévin helped to set the table. Delighted by the unexpected snack–time, he ogled the golden madeleines. Mrs Préau sat at the end of the table, facing the living room, with her back to the French doors that overlooked the garden.

She was paralysed by nerves. The muffled sound of small knocks kept getting through to her, but nobody else seemed to be able to hear them. Outside, night began to fall. Cutting the cake, Mr Desmoulins nodded his head.

'An apple tart – you're really too kind. Blandine loves it.'

'Yes, it's my favourite. Laurie, come to the table, please.'

Reluctantly, the girl left her cartoon and took her place. The only one missing was the stone boy.

'And you, Mr Desmoulins, what's your favourite dessert?'

The man put down the long kitchen knife and picked up a cake knife.

'Oh, I don't eat dessert, I'm diabetic. No sweets! May I?'

Mrs Préau blanched. She hadn't thought of that. Fortunately, there was cider. Provided he would give in to alcohol . . .

'Yes, it's very annoying,' stressed Mrs Desmoulins, holding a plate for the surprise guest. 'Philippe doesn't drink alcohol, either.'

'Apart from a beer from time to time.'

'Yes, well, a little at night.'

Mrs Préau's heart quickened. Her plan was turning into a fiasco. A piece of tart was handed to her.

'No thank you,' she said. 'There is cinnamon on this part of the tart, and I'm not supposed to have any because of my high blood pressure. But I'd gladly take a piece without.'

Mr Desmoulins gave the portion sprinkled with cinnamon to his wife and served Mrs Préau, joking about the disadvantages of age when it came to health and dietary restrictions. Then he handed the madeleines to the children and offered cider to his wife and neighbour. Both agreed and, finally, he was tempted himself, to Mrs Préau's great relief.

'It won't kill me,' he said jokingly.

Mrs Préau did not touch the glass but ate her tart. Laurie's mother had another cider, which she found 'a wonderful little taste of the countryside, or hay', and the children feasted on madeleines. They were allowed to leave the table quickly, and were now dozing on the sofa in front of an episode of *Barbapapa*. Mr Desmoulins, who hadn't touched a thing but had drained his glass of cider, was recounting how he had designed the house, creating a garage/studio with removable sliding panel curtains, which he had installed himself on all the doors and windows to the ground and then demolished the hundred-year-old boundary wall damaged by ivy and replaced it with sturdy latticed concrete. Mrs Préau pretended to be interested in what he had to say, but it was hard to concentrate.

Granny Elsa . . . Granny Elsa . . .

In her head, with the regularity of a metronome, the sound of knocking against a wooden wall in the kitchen was getting slowly louder. Mrs Desmoulins seemed lost in her thoughts, batting her eyelashes gently. She realised that night was falling when she saw the garden in darkness, and called the children. It was bath time. But nothing stirred on the couch. On the TV, the cartoon had given way to ads. She got up, in pain.

'Laurie, Kévin, come on, get up,' she stammered.

Mrs Desmoulins wavered. Her husband hardly paid her any attention. He was drawing an invisible floorplan of the foundations of the house with his index finger on the tablecloth, searching for his words, as if in slow motion. Mrs Préau saw Laurie's mum take five or six steps before collapsing. This time, her husband turned around. With a limp hand, Mrs Desmoulins tried in vain to grab the arm of the couch.

'Blandine?'

Mrs Préau met his incredulous gaze.

'Your wife isn't feeling well,' she observed.

Her husband leapt up and walked over to his wife to help her up. Mrs Desmoulins was groggy.

'The children ...' she said just before she lost consciousness.

The man looked up at the couch: sprawled in the middle of the cushions, Kévin and Laurie seemed to be deeply asleep.

He didn't understand right away how dramatic a scene was playing out in his house.

He didn't understand it when he saw Mrs Préau stand to face him with a hammer.

'Damned diabetes!' he grumbled with regret.

50

Come on, Granny Elsa, kill him!

Mr Desmoulins saved his life with a reflex, raising one arm to protect his face. The hammer crashed down on his left forearm, which was horrifically painful.

'What's the matter with you?'

Mrs Préau struck his arm three times before realising that she would never manage it with this hammer. Panicked, the old woman recoiled as far as the table. She hadn't foreseen this.

I'm here, Granny Elsa!

Sweat beaded on her nose. Bastien's voice clanged in her head. Mrs Préau closed her eyes for a few seconds.

Get a hold of yourself.

Do it, no matter what.

Save the child.

She'd use the kitchen knife.

'What are you doing? Are you crazy?'

The man, who had fallen back on the tiles, was now trying to get back up. But his body wasn't reacting like he wanted it to. His legs bowed beneath him. The Stilnox mixed with cider had had some effect on his body.

'What's wrong with Blandine and the kids?'

The old woman came back over to him, her hair a mess, holding the knife and hammer in front of her.

'Where is he?' she demanded.

Mr Desmoulins crawled to the sofa, where he pulled himself up with difficulty between the children. He groaned between each word.

'What did . . . what did you put in your cakes?'

Help, Granny Elsa!

Mrs Préau's gaze vacillated between the kitchen and the living room. She stamped her feet.

'Where is he?' she insisted.

The man checked his children's breathing, shaking their motionless little bodies. The groaning gave way to rage.

'You've poisoned my children!'

'The dose of sleeping tablets in the madeleines was too weak to kill them – but I'm no expert on the subject,' she qualified.

Mr Desmoulins screamed. He sprang up from the sofa with the intention of hurling himself on the old woman, but fell onto his knees at the first step. Mrs Préau moved back towards the kitchen, still brandishing her two weapons in front of her.

'Calm down!'

'You drugged all of us! I don't understand ... you had some too ...'

His eyes rested on the tart. He could clearly see the part dusted in cinnamon that his wife had eaten. You didn't have to be too clever to see which part hid the sleeping tablets.

'I did this for the little boy,' Mrs Préau argued, 'because you're filth, and so is your wife ... and because no one wants to believe me, starting with those two bitches at the social welfare centre!'

She glanced at the sofa.

'And those two are in on it, too.'

Granny Elsa! Granny Elsa!

In the kitchen, the knocking became twice as strong. The child was there, right there. Mrs Préau trembled with fear. The handle of the hammer slid in her damp palm. Mr Desmoulins got back up with difficulty.

'Is this the boy in the garden, again? It was you who made a complaint to social services? That's why you came here? You've completely cracked!'

I'm here, Granny Elsa! I'm here!

The old woman turned to the right where a broom cupboard stood about a metre and a half tall. She struck the door with the hammer. The noises in her head stopped instantly.

'Is that where you hid the boy? Is he your son?'

The man tried twice as hard to stay upright.

'I only have one son, and that's Kévin.'

'So it must be a child you kidnapped.'

'You're nothing but a senile old woman.'

Without breaking her gaze with the man, Mrs Préau pulled sharply at the door. It opened. Was the child being held there, in darkness? Mr Desmoulins came towards the kitchen, reeling.

'Stay where you are!' she ordered.

Mrs Préau peered inside.

Nothing.

Nothing but rows and rows of jam.

The husband let out a feeble laugh.

'You found the kid? That's the house speciality: preserved little boy!'

Furious, Mrs Préau couldn't breathe. With her hammer, she cleared out all the jam to get to the back of the cupboard.

Don't leave me, Granny Elsa. Don't leave me!

The man was less than two metres from Mrs Préau.

'There's nothing in that cupboard! You won't find a thing.'

'He's there, behind ... I'm certain of it ... There's a false back, is that it?'

Mrs Préau hit the inside of the cupboard with her hammer. It sounded hollow. Her face lit up.

'Bastien? Are you there?'

She hit harder and faster, gouging the chipboard.

'It's me! It's Granny Elsa!'

Granny Elsa never saw the man throw himself at her in a last-ditch effort.

Cruel stars.
Thousands of yellow stars.
I can't die.
Not now.
Bastien! Bastien!

CAN'T BELIEVE YOUR EYES

'He who accepts evil without fighting against it collaborates with it.'

Francis Bacon

51

The phone rang at about seven thirty. Martin had to interrupt his consultation and leave his patient sitting on the examination table for a moment with his shirt rolled up under his armpits. Dr Préau couldn't immediately identify the speaker on the other end of the line. It was a thick voice, and the speaker seemed out of breath.

'It's Isabelle, your mother's housekeeper. You should come, Dr Préau, your mother might be in trouble.'

'What are you saying?'

'It's because of the shutters.'

'The shutters?'

'The shutters on her house – she hasn't closed them. It's not normal.'

Martin sighed. He'd just done two back-to-back house

calls for two probable cases of swine flu. He didn't have time to waste on some story about shutters.

'Have you been to see her?'

'Dr Préau, I rang the bell but no one answered. We tried, me and my husband, to open the door, but the key wouldn't go into the lock.'

'What are you talking about?'

'The police are there, Dr Préau. You should come right away. Something has happened at the neighbours' house.'

'What does this have to do with my mother?'

The housekeeper hesitated for a moment.

'I'm not sure, but I think that your mum . . . she went to their house.'

A memory of a conversation from Sunday came back to the doctor. He cleared his throat.

Dr Martin Préau wrapped up his consultation briskly, practically pushing the patient out the door. He threw his bag on the desk and took out an envelope that had been hastily torn open. Inside, there was an old postcard with a picture of Rue des Lilas in 1925, such as it was – a vague dirt path through fenced-off gardens. On the back of the card, his mother apologised to him. When he had read the words written in a careful hand, he knew that they had been deliberately chosen in keeping with his mother's perennial rambling logic. The message had now taken on another meaning entirely.

He put on his duffel coat, closed the office and, a moment later, pulled out of the Boulevard de l'Ouest at the wheel of his Peugeot 307 at 70 kilometres per hour.

So long as she hadn't done it again.

He saw his mother's pale face in a courtroom, eight years before. The thinness of her body. And her determination to be convicted.

. . . My neighbours . . . as I tried to tell you, they hit one of their sons. You know how sensitive a subject violence against children is for me. . .

Why go to the neighbours'?

What was she hoping for?

Martin's greatest fear had always been finding his mother at the bottom of the stairs one day. At her age, the slightest fall could bring on a loss of mobility. That she was still capable not only of dressing herself, doing her own shopping and cooking her own meals, but also of managing a budget for herself, meant that he could put off the idea of her being placed in a medicalised facility. With crutches or a wheelchair, staying in a two-storey house became out of the question. A fracture was tantamount to a one-way ticket to the hospice. And with her CV, she'd end up in an Alzheimer's ward on Tiapridal, her brain turned to mush, being fed through a straw – but all that was nothing in comparison with what might re-emerge from her past.

Driving along Allée Victor Hugo, Martin swore.

He knew it.

He just didn't want to see it.

His mother had stopped taking her medication and he hadn't reacted.

A fit of dementia, a psychotic episode . . .

Had she attacked someone?

He hit the steering wheel with his fist. Dr Préau didn't have very much faith in himself. Growing up without a father limits your self-confidence. At that moment, he felt like he was going through all of his exams, naked, in a lecture hall, with all his classmates pointing. A carer with no balls. Martin hadn't had the courage to commit his mother to being hospitalised. To occupy his mind, as he did after each visit he made to 6 Rue des Lilas, he listed off the best care facilities in the region. Martin reached the neighbourhood near the train station before finishing up his list. Two ambulances were double-parked on Rue des Lilas. A police car was blocking off the road. The doctor parked his car along the railway line, turned off the ignition and grabbed his bag, which he had thrown on the back seat in haste. The slam of the car door startled him. He walked briskly to the fieldstone house with the slate roof that stood taller than the other houses, insolent. He was stopped in his tracks by a policeman, who changed his mind when Martin identified himself as a doctor. He crossed a second barrier that ran down the street, made up of a dozen neighbours. He got the feeling that, among the older ones, some were staring at him, hostile. Among them, Isabelle, freezing in a shawl, stood clutching her husband.

Martin reached the first ambulance. One of the back doors of the vehicle was open. With some apprehension, he ventured a glance, looking for the frail silhouette of an old woman on a stretcher, but two paramedics were in the way.

'Excuse me, I'm Dr Préau. I think my mother had an accident . . . '

The nurse turned to him and looked him over quickly before pointing with her head.

'You should go down there.'

Furtively, Martin glanced at a boy and a little girl lying in the ambulance, aged between three and six, he guessed, oxygen masks on their faces. He felt like he was looking at Bastien again, in intensive care in the A&E at Montfermeil.

'Sorry!'

The doctor stepped back, the door narrowly missing closing on his nose. The siren filled the street with its grim cry. What had happened to the kids he had seen in the ambulance?

What you took for a delusion is unfortunately only the truth.

Martin put the collar of his coat up and walked in the direction he had been shown, towards the fieldstone house. The shutters on the ground floor were open like the housekeeper had said. No sign of life. It was across the road that the forces of order were at work behind a concrete fence, a family home that his mother suspected of being a place of abuse. Martin stopped in the middle of the street.

Could it be that she had been right?

Dr Mamnoue has been aware of it for several weeks. I have also alerted social services, and I made an official statement to the police on Friday.

The screech of the fire engine siren startled him. The emergency vehicle was going down the one-way road in the wrong direction.

'Sir, you can't stay there.'

The policeman came up to him nervously. Martin identified himself.

'You're the son of the woman who lives across the road?'

'Yes.'

The officer grabbed his radio. The conversation was brief.

'Stay here, please, sir. We'll come back to you.'

'What happened? Is my mother in that house?'

'I can't tell you anything. You have to wait here.'

The iron gate swung open sharply to allow a stretcher through. The officer forced Martin to move back on the path. Under the shock blanket was an unknown blonde woman between thirty-five and forty, her face half-covered by a mask. The doctor shuddered.

Supported by two police officers, a stocky man of about the same age appeared framed by the gate. He had one arm in a sling and his green sweatshirt was stained with blood. Pale under the lamp, he looked at the stretcher as it moved away.

The doctor felt a tingling in his fingertips.

He pressed his back against the wall.

Again, forgive me for causing you all this upset.

Damn it!

What kind of shitstorm had she got herself into?

52

Sitting on a chair with a frayed cobalt-blue fabric back, the man watched his hands. Usually soft and warm regardless of the season – a physical characteristic appreciated by his patients and Audrette – they were particularly damp and cool. His fingers shook in spite of his efforts to control his nerves.

Martin pulled up the wrist of his right shirtsleeve. His watch read nine o'clock. Lieutenant Sevran was with a colleague. Their voices spilled through the open office door to him in the hallway. Sevran had found an indication of proceedings against one Elsa Préau on a list of people interviewed as part of a criminal investigation. He had asked for whatever might be pulled up from the archives for the case, which dated back to 1997. And then a policeman stopped in to see him, the one he was chatting with in the corridor.

Knees together, shoulders hunched, Martin ignored the nagging hunger in his stomach. But he was cold without his duffel coat – despite the prevailing heat in the police station. Through habit, rather than through fear of saying too much, he kept his teeth clenched. Seeing his mother lying on the floor in a pool of blood with three guys over her, trying to revive her, had made him tense.

People think doctors can take anything.

They didn't bother with the kid gloves when they painted the picture for him.

Pelvic fracture, major internal injuries with bilateral damage to the lobes of the lungs and a concussion. The neighbour, that 90-kilo mass in a sweatshirt he'd spotted earlier, had reduced his dear mum to a pulp when he hurled himself at her, her head striking the edge of the kitchen counter in the fall. They kept the most vital prognosis for last. Martin's mother was in a coma. This just rekindled old memories. Only this time, she might not come back.

His phone vibrated in his coat pocket. Audrette sent a text message to her husband to comfort him. She missed Martin. He missed her arms, her breasts pressed around his skull, cutting off any morbid thoughts. He imagined the house, a glass of Bordeaux in hand, standing in front of the bay window overlooking the sloping garden. The view across the hills above the city, a panorama they hadn't grown tired of four years later. A house bought on credit, too big for the two of them, and which they tried in vain to fill with the unbearable screaming of a baby adored by its young parents as an affirmation of life. Martin had quickly phoned Audrette from the police car to tell her what had just happened, foreseeing that he'd be late returning home.

'You're her guardian! Shit! You know what she's capable of. Why did you not have her put in care? Do you realise what the consequences of this could be? If the children and their mother don't come out of this, how do you think it will go?'

The first reaction of his wife was violent and had crushed him. When Audrette called in tears, vowing that if her mother-in-law was doing it a second time, it would drive her to the madhouse, he regained a bit of courage.

His mother, his burden.

If there were a single reason that Martin had returned from Canada, disregarding his education and a great career that awaited him there in the cardiac department headed by his father, it was his mum. Only for his mum. The letters that he received from France were miserable. With no brother or sister, her mother dead, her father terminally ill with cancer, she had only him left, her son. Miserable letters, but entertaining ones. Her letters covered her reading, her bizarre diets, her students' imaginings and the unlikely animals she collected in her garden, but also French social policy, the problems created by globalisation and ecological disasters. More recently, in a letter dated 6 January 2006, commenting on the work of an economist, she was already foreseeing a stock market crash in the United States, the repercussions of which would be global. Of her solitude, however, she said nothing, or very little, quoting a line about the melancholy that seized at dusk, after her schooldays filled with screaming children. So the young man, his heart shrivelled up by remorse, guilty of having neglected his mother to be with the father who had abandoned him on the other side of the world, returned to France. A hiatus of eight years, in the middle of which, Audrette blossomed like a flower.

Martin surveyed the narrow, cluttered room: on the lower cabinet, a SWAT helmet resting on a stack of files, and safes, similar to those found in the hotel room, set the tone. Hung on the wall were a coat, a child's drawing and a photograph of four smiling men, their arms around each others' necks – Lieutenant Sevran's team. So you could be happy in the police, have a few beers and be chummy for the camera. The child's drawing brought back memories of two police sergeants standing in his doctor's surgery. One of the officers, who had a cold, pulled a handkerchief from his pocket to clear his sinuses, drowning out the announcement of Bastien and Granny Elsa's 'accident' in a tissue.

Back then, there were also children's drawings on the walls of his surgery.

Bastien's drawings.

All this came back to him now.

'I have nothing to add, sir,' his mother had whispered before the guards took her. The 'diabolical grandmother' would make the front page of the *Parisien* again.

A dangerous grandmother – but is she crazy?

Psychiatrists have it out at the trial of Elsa Préau, accused of killing her grandson, age 7.

Georges Milhau
Special correspondent

A question haunts the court. A key issue. Should Elsa Préau, who has been on trial for the past three days, be in a courtroom? Was she or was she not accountable when, on 6 June 1997, she led her grandson Bastien into the town park, sat down with him under a tree and administered a dose of sedatives sufficient to kill him? The three experts who examined him do not agree. The case, which is already complicated, is awash in confusion. For Dr Valente, the accused is paranoid, suffering from delusions and an obsessive fixation on Bastien, but the delirium does not affect other areas of her mind. In this state of 'mental precariousness, she has become progressively convinced of the torture inflicted on Bastien by his mother'. For him, Elsa Préau's responsibility is moderately diminished. But for Dr Dupin, Elsa Préau suffered a paranoid psychotic breakdown. His conclusion is unequivocal: 'This crime is not judicable and does not warrant a criminal verdict.' According to the third expert, Dr Texier, we are dealing with a paranoid personality, a pathological one, with a 'hypertrophied ego' and a quasi-symbiotic relationship with Bastien. The total effect 'impaired her judgement and took control of her actions at the time in question', but it did not render the accused responsible.

The jurors are lost, particularly since the accused absolutely insists on being tried and convicted, and doesn't want to hear a word said about mental illness. She insists on 'appearing before Martin (her son) to answer for her heinous act'. Dr Texier has taken this reaction to be a further sign of Elsa Préau's paranoia.

With so many uncertainties, what followed the parade of witnesses yesterday seemed quite preposterous. We heard that Elsa Préau, 62 years old today, has had an exceptional life. Her intelligence and unrivalled tenacity propelled her from her position as a school teacher to headmistress, where she became known by reputation all the way up to the Ministry of Education for creating the first 'nature and garden' class in 1991. It was also heard that she had loved her son Martin too much, and that her descent into paranoia began when she discovered bruises on Bastien's body, and especially when her daughter-in-law Audrette forbade her from seeing her grandson on the advice of a juvenile court judge. Elsa Préau then tried to alert numerous people around her, convinced that her grandson was a victim of abuse. She even sent a letter to the director of the County Council that runs social services. But no one believed her.

Then the police officer who interrogated her in custody entered. He had allowed her to 'confess', which had lasted all night. 'She imagined Bastien to be suffering so.' She did not think she would be capable of living without her grandson. Denied visits with Bastien, she wanted to die, but could not bring herself to leave the child alone with his mother. 'She administered what was a fatal dose to Bastien, but insufficient for herself. She failed.' Finally, the officer stated that, until that point, 'nobody had listened to her', not even her son Martin, whose refusal to listen she did not understand. 'So she turned herself in.'

Closing remarks from both sides and the verdict are expected today.

The lieutenant turned his computer screen so that the man in front of him could read the article he had found online.

'Does that refresh your memory at all, Doctor?'

Martin grimaced. He needed more time. It was all happening too fast. Barely four hours had passed since the assault and his mother had already gone from victim to the guilty party. Lieutenant Sevran took on a contrite air.

'The policeman mentioned in the paper is our captain. He thinks that he saw your mother when she came in to file her report for our logbook last Monday. Our social worker had taken Mrs Préau's statement very seriously, you know ... The captain remembered her face, but hadn't made the connection with the trial.'

He put a flabby hand to his chin.

'Ten years ago ... I was a sergeant in Nantes ...'

The officer turned the screen back around on its pedestal.

'Let's look further back ...'

Martin's voice rose over the clacking of the keyboard.

'Have you had any news about the children?'

'Not yet.'

'And the parents? What about the father? Did my mother hurt him badly?'

'Mr Desmoulins is in custody. He's being considered as part of the investigation.' The officer sighed. 'Ah! *Voilà*! "Killer grandmother judged not responsible: accused is acquitted." That's why there's no record of a conviction on the system.'

The screen rotated a second time. Martin went back to looking at his shoes.

There was no reason for him to read it.

He remembered perfectly the reports of the trial that appeared in the press, describing his mother as a wild-looking woman, detached from the world around her.

He could still hear them reading out the charge.

'I have never seen distress or despair register on your face, madam. I don't understand you. I don't understand what makes you tick.'

The lawyer then started in on an interminable and confusing monologue, painting a picture of an 'abominable act' committed by an 'egotistical, egocentric' woman, returning constantly to his failure to understand the crime and its motive. Why would he deny the despair that brought a grandmother to murder her grandson? A despair that drove her to lunacy, fed by the recent loss of her father from cancer, despair about which all the experts agreed. Why deny Bastien's troubles and physical injuries that were worrying his grandmother when they were real? No. He took it out on the retired school teacher.

'Truly diabolical!'

When the prosecutor mocked Martin by reducing him to the level of 'a little boy at his mummy's apron strings', and basically accused him of perjury, the doctor was then sunk into guilt.

Guilty of having prescribed the Tranxene, which she had hidden in the cake designed to kill her and Bastien alike.

Not worthy to bear his father's name.

Five hundred pills, reduced to a powder.

And she survived after ten days in a coma.

An irritated cough shook Martin from his thoughts. The lieutenant was watching him, his arms crossed.

'There's one thing that I'm having trouble understanding, Doctor,' he said softly. 'After what your mother did to you, how could you continue to see her? Is it possible to forgive someone for killing your son, even if it is your mother?'

Martin looked up at the lieutenant.

'People always imagine that, for a doctor, it's easier to accept a serious illness in your family, that your experience will protect you from the power of your emotions. It's nothing like that. It's not written in any manual how to tell your mother that her grandson is suffering from leukaemia and that his fever, the paleness of his skin and the bruises on his body are the effects of a relapse.'

'You hid the fact that your son had cancer from your mother?'

Martin smiled bitterly.

'No one in the family knew other than Audrette and me. Bastien thought we were giving him a treatment to supplement the calcium in his bones. After his chemo, we went to Corsica for three months to wait for his hair to grow back. We still believed in a cure. Then he got worse ... Do you know what the likelihood of survival is in a child whose acute lymphoblastic leukaemia has relapsed?'

The lieutenant shook his head, thrown. The doctor's eyes shone with tears.

'Thirty per cent. In Bastien's case, with a serious case of the disease, the prognosis dropped to fifteen per cent. Six weeks, two months at the absolute max. He was already suffering. Without knowing it, my mother spared him the relentlessness of the medics and the ordeal that awaited him.'

Sevran shook his head and looked up at the wall where a child's drawing was taped.

Martin guessed exactly what the man must be thinking.

If it were my son, I would have bet on the fifteen per cent.

One night, at the onset of his illness, Bastien woke his parents up, screaming. A cry of terror that Martin would never forget. In his nightmare, a witch was pulling out his hair. He was holding his head, crippled with pain. His hair fell out two days later.

In keeping quiet the reasons for Bastien's deteriorating health, Martin and Audrette had planted a seed in the already fragile mind of his Granny Elsa, and her psychosis swelled to breaking point. Like a castaway lost in the middle of the ocean grasping a life jacket, Martin still held on to the idea that she had saved his son from the worst.

53

Audrette was sleeping on her side, her head half-buried in the pillow held tightly in her arms.

Like every night, she woke up at two in the morning. After shuffling to the toilet and drinking a few sips of water from the tap, she returned to bed, pressing her chest against her husband's bare back in the hope that the contact would give her better dreams.

Martin looked at her face in the light of day. In the duvet, her waist cut a valley dominated by the voluptuous curves of her hips. Her shoulder-length hair, coiled at the neck, reflected glints of amber.

He desired his wife as much as always, with the same fervour, the same addiction. But Martin doubted that Audrette still wanted him.

Since the return of Mrs Préau after ten years in a nursing home in Hyères, Audrette resented the relationship that his mother had renewed with her son. Their relationship was strained. The last memory she had of her mother-in-law was that of a woman sitting in the dock, saying softly to the court: 'My daughter-in-law is completely ignorant of the evil she carries in her. That is why I am so indulgent of her.' The tragedy of Martin. Who was to blame? In 1988, hadn't he played a dirty trick on his mother by coming back from Montreal with a little surprise – a foreigner with a ridiculous name? How could you commit such a blunder as the only son of a divorced mother? She wasn't best pleased that Martin had been seeing his girlfriend since university, that she was an agricultural engineer and very pretty.

The birth of Bastien had signalled an end to hostilities. Granny Elsa, struck dumb with happiness, would even have smoked the peace pipe and had lunch at McDonald's with her daughter-in-law if asked.

Nothing could happen to Bastien.

There should not be bruises on his skin.

Granny Elsa had succumbed to panic. She needed a scapegoat. A scapegoat not related to her by blood.

After Bastien's death, Audrette had gone back to be with her family in Canada – a desperate fugue, a penance. Her return to France years later was accompanied by a requirement: that Martin cut all ties with his mother. Of this, he was not capable.

The couple's long separation, however, had helped to heal some of Martin's wounds. He gave up his one-night stands, his addiction to alcohol and Xanax. He gained enough courage to rebuild his clientele, strangely thin on the ground after his mother's trial, left the family home where he had seen fit to take refuge after Audrette's departure and ordered a plane ticket to Montreal online.

Martin could not live without this woman's love. He didn't flinch when they found themselves face to face, in Beijing, a small Szechuan restaurant in Chinatown with large coloured windows that contrasted with the chalky white drifts heaped on the footpaths. In this welcoming room where burning hotplates overflowed with Singapore noodles, he confessed that Bastien deserved better from his parents. Neither should ever forget him, they who must obey his dearest wish: that Bastien should become a big brother. After two ice-cold beers, their fingers inter-twined again. A little more time was needed before they could shed their modesty. Nevertheless, ever since their first attempted reunion Audrette's belly refused to oblige. As the days passed, making love became a source of anxiety and apprehension. Each month, Audrette lived through a day of 'menstrual mourning'. And although Martin desired his wife constantly, sex became rare. Recent events had not been brought to any conclusion.

Martin closed his eyes to still his pathetic impulse.

He kissed the oval of her shoulder, stroked his sleeping wife's hair, and went down to the kitchen to drop a capsule into the espresso machine, failing to listen to the *France Info* news.

Before going to his office, he would visit his mother in the hospital as he had taken to doing over the past week. For fifteen minutes, he contemplated a bruised body supported by a shell, her neck set in a disproportionately large collar, the mouthpiece of a respirator filling her lips. In his hands, his mother's felt sometimes warm, and sometimes cold. Mrs Préau was still holding back in the face of death, plunged into an irreversible coma.

54

Martin knew all about the power of the prosecution. His mother had bitter experience of it. It was because of a judge's stubbornness that Mrs Préau had to sit in the dock, even though according to the initial psychiatric assessments from the beginning of the case, it was clear that it was no place for her.

'You have to understand,' said Sevran, nodding as if to apologise. 'A history like this is just fodder to the prosecutor. He has it in his head that the law won't make the same mistake twice.'

A smell of stale cigarette smoke emanated from a leather jacket hanging on a peg on the wall. The officer sat behind his desk, looking exhausted as if it were the morning after a drunken night. Between his fingers, an odd mug bearing the image of Chupa Chups lollipops turned slowly. His hair, styled in spikes, formed a small, glossy, light brown brush, which narrowed towards the top of his face. His purplish rectangular glasses frames which matched his shirt, worn under a black and white jacquard jumper, advertised his nonconformist nature. The lieutenant looked more like a holiday resort rep and ex-fan of Madness and the Specials than one of those narrow-minded cops that abound on TV series.

'The law didn't make a mistake,' said Martin.

'Each to their own. I'm not taking sides.'

'Is this why you called me in this morning? Because I have my first appointment in less than half an hour . . . '

'I called you in, Doctor, regarding the logbook entry that reports suspected abuse – which is in the book of evidence for the case. This is a line of inquiry that we need to explore, even though it is a priori closed.'

'Excuse me?'

The officer pushed the mug against the mouse pad on his computer. The pad was a questionable grey, covered in coffee stains.

'I mean that despite the psychiatric profile of the victim and her past, the assumption is that there's no smoke without fire. Also, we conducted a required inter-view with a number of people . . . '

Lieutenant Sevran threw a folder in front of him and turned its pages rapidly with the weariness of a notary.

'... Among them were two social workers, the teacher of the Blaise Pascal School whom your mother visited, her psychiatrist Dr Mamnoue ... Do you know him?'

'Yes. He's been taking care of my mother for years.'

'That's what he said to us. We also interviewed the housekeeper, the home care nurse and her nearest neighbours on Rue des Lilas. The Desmoulins children ...'

'How are they?'

'They're well. Their mother has also pulled through.'

Martin tore a bit of the nail off his right thumb. His nails had become seriously shorter over the last ten days, and now he was attacking his cuticles. Elsewhere, a beard was beginning to eat up his cheeks.

'Good.' He sighed.

'They were lucky.'

'Yes.'

'And your mother too, I mean ...'

'Yes. It's lucky she didn't kill anyone.'

'This is it. So, the Desmoulins children and their mother have also been interviewed in the course of the inquiry.'

The dossier closed in a single movement. The lieutenant placed his elbows on it and joined his hands together.

'All the witnesses agree on one point, Doctor: your mother suspected that something wasn't right at her neighbours' place, and she tried to warn people about a case of maltreatment, and no one believed her.'

'I didn't believe her either.'

'She talked to you about it?'

'Very briefly.'

'When was that?'

'Sunday, the twenty-fifth of October, I think. She called me because she wasn't well. She was overcome. My mother said that it was "a question of life or death". I left my house in a state. And when I arrived, she had calmed down.'

'Why the change of mood?'

Martin tensed.

'I think she'd taken a Stilnox.'

'The sleeping pills found in the madeleines. Did you prescribe it for her?'

'Yes' Martin sighed. 'You already asked me that question the night of the assault. She was taking it because she was having trouble sleeping.'

'And what happened next?'

'I'm the one who got annoyed. She had given me such a fright . . . And I came all the way over for nothing!'

'So, on that occasion, she spoke to you about a mistreated child at the neighbours'?'

'I think so. I remember that she was making a connection between the telemarketing calls she kept receiving and the neighbour across the way who worked for a company that did . . . window installations.'

'She felt threatened?'

'Yes.'

'And you didn't take that threat seriously?'

Martin tapped his fingertips on his lips.

'You know as much as I do about her paranoia and her hallucinations. When she started talking about a child who looked like Bastien, I . . . I lost it.'

'You lost it.'

'Yes.'

Martin sat up in his chair.

'It has been more than ten years since Bastien died. Ten years that my mother has been asking after him. Every phone call, every letter ended with "and how is my little Bastien?"'

'The child, according to her, looked like your deceased son?' the lieutenant asked, perplexed.

'Yes,' answered Martin.

'When you were at her house, did she show you the child through her bedroom window?'

'No.'

The lieutenant leaned on his desk. He tried to read the name that appeared on a vibrating mobile phone. Finally, he let the phone ring out without answering and took up the Chupa Chups mug again.

'At the present moment, Doctor, other than your mother, no one has ever seen other children at the Desmoulins' besides the two little ones who are in the hospital. And that's all we've got. No third child in the record, no child of previous marriages, nothing.'

Martin stared at the red artwork on the mug.

'It's a Dalí, that.'

'What?'

'On your mug. The Chupa Chups logo. It was designed by Salvador Dalí.'

The lieutenant turned the mug towards him.

'It was a present from my daughter for Father's Day,' he said, with vague tenderness.

Suddenly, the officer froze. He opened one of his desk drawers and stuck his hand in, rummaging for a piece of paper he soon found.

'That's not right, what I told you – we do have something on the little boy.'

He showed Martin a photocopy of a drawing in a clear plastic sleeve.

'It's the work of the little Desmoulins girl. You can clearly see that she's drawn something there, under what looks like a tree. She told us that she wanted to draw a doll, then a dog, and then she talked about an imaginary friend, her brother's, and then she started crying because she didn't remember any more. Basically, we don't really know if she's telling the truth, or if she's drawn something real. Frankly, we didn't want to push it too much. That's it. That's all we've got.'

Martin crossed his arms, then scratched his forehead, embarrassed.

'In her last letter, she talked about a photo . . .'

'Your mother wrote you a letter?' gawped the lieutenant.

'Yes.'

'In which she broke the news that the child existed?'

'Yes.'

'Would it be possible for you to bring it in to me?'
Martin opened his bag and took out the envelope. The
lieutenant read it, readjusting his glasses.

'That confirms the statement made by Ms Tremblay,
our social worker. Your mother received a call from her
on the twenty-sixth of October ... and mentioned a
camera ...'

'Did you say Valérie Tremblay?' asked Martin timidly.

'Yes, you know her, is that right?'

The doctor had a fleeting vision of a body undressing
in his surgery, and adorable little breasts offered up for
examination.

'She was one of my patients. When I knew her, she ran
the support service at a halfway house in Chelles. Does
she work here?'

'Yes. She has been seconded to the station, and I have
to say she's been a huge help to us. Do you mind if I keep
it?'

'Sorry?'

'The letter,' the lieutenant said. 'Would you like a
photocopy?'

Martin shook his head.

He was late for his appointments.

He couldn't wait to forget about his Stilnox prescriptions turned weapons in a crime, to overlook his lack of good judgement more generally, and in particular, to erase the image of the social worker's breasts, with nipples as round as Chupa Chups.

55

Martin's shoes left prints on the wet floor, ephemeral signposts leading to the centre of Raincy-Montfermeil Hospital's intensive care unit. When he entered the room, already equipped with a protective mask, a medical gown and polypropylene overshoes, the humming machines that kept the patient alive assailed his ears. The doctor approached the bed cautiously, peered into his mother's face, then leaned over to caress her brow, banging a knee against a metal bar on the bed. His mother's shrivelled skin criss-crossed with veins reminded him of crossing the snow in the spring, when valiant blades of grass poke through the ice. Without a word, he took a seat on a chair to the right of the window, crossed his legs and leaned his head against the wall. A fine rain was caressing the glass. The atmosphere in the room matched the 11 November weather, filled with commemorations to sad figures, idiot ministers too dapper to hear, much less make sense of, the cries of war. Martin had an aversion to death and its celebrations. His allergy to memory grew with every autumn. Martin would rush to the video shop to rent all the films available, to fill the nights and the hours of that day when, abandoned to her melancholy, Audrette would forget to smile. He then stood an army of beer cans on the living-room coffee table, smiling at zombie massacres, unflinchingly witnessing the flood of blood as mafiosi settled their scores, and sleeping like a baby, neck bent back on the sofa in front of Cameron Diaz and Jude Law in a romantic comedy, half-naked in a bed.

'Excuse me! I didn't know there was anyone here.'

The doctor sat up in his chair. Dr Mamnoue stood in the doorway. He was wearing the same medical gown as Martin, and was about to put the protective mask on his face.

'Hello, Doctor.'

'Ah! It's you, Martin, I didn't recognise you with your mask. Are you growing a beard?'

The old man came a few steps closer, and they shook hands. Dr Mamnoue was taking advantage of his day off to come and visit Mrs Préau.

'How is she?'

'Stable.'

Martin didn't comment further. Both knew that Elsa Préau was going to a better place. The doctor in turn went to the patient. He tried to warm his hands, then smiled and spoke softly to her: Dr Mamnoue apologised for not having come earlier, he regretted that he wouldn't be seeing her every Wednesday at his office.

'I miss you, Elsa. I'm very sad about what's happened to you.'

Upset, Martin turned towards the window.

How he envied this man's capacity for tenderness and kindness.

Not once since the attack had Martin managed to speak to his mother.

Would he ever be able to express his feelings?

Leaning on a teak counter in front of a drinks dispenser, stripped of their protective gear, the two men shared a similar malaise: feeling blameworthy for not having foreseen the danger, and for not having intervened earlier. Martin had inherited a double penalty, having twice missed his mother's insanity. He was also the only one to put sugar in his coffee. Dr Mamnoue, anxious, shared his thoughts.

'The strange figure of the child appeared very early in our sessions. From mid-August. She had noticed that the child never played with his brother and sister, and that bothered her. At the time, she was also obsessed with the dust and dirt caused by lorries passing on her road. I didn't really give much attention to this story about the neighbours. And then, in September, there was this dream that she told me about . . . ' The old man pulled lightly on the collar of his shirt, clearing his throat.

'There was mention of Bastien. Or rather, that's what I understood. But now, I would lean towards the idea of her having seen – or imagined – a child in the neighbours' garden.'

Martin swallowed his coffee in small sips; it was so bitter that despite the huge amount of sugar, it rasped at his taste buds.

'What was the dream?' he asked.

'I took notes after the session, it was so frightening: a child was playing your mother's piano in the middle of the night. Elsa came down from her room in the dark. In the room, a window was "fighting" with the wind, and the curtains were "angry". And when the child turned around to her, there was dirt on his face and in his mouth.'

'Terrifying.'

'As you say, "terra-fying".'

'Weren't you worried that my mother was having such anxieties?'

The old man raised his eyebrows, surprised.

'Your mother was always burdened with anxieties, Martin. And her nightmares, believe you me, are much more shocking than those films where they torture people with vegetable peelers or sewing machines. This one was unusual insofar as it was the first in which, in some way, it seemed that your mother had taken on board the idea that her grandson was dead.'

'The presence of soil in his mouth . . .'

'Exactly! And that was very encouraging after years spent in denial. Why would I have been alarmed?' Dr Mamnoue picked up his coffee. His hand was shaking. 'Hmmf! This coffee would raise the dead.'

Martin managed a smile.

'Did my mother tell you about other dreams?'

The man shook his head.

'Elsa started to shut herself off at the beginning of October. We would speak about subjects of little importance, her worries about the telephone, her new diet . . . Then there was that flu that she recovered from so well. And then you called me to say that you suspected that she had stopped taking her medication.'

'That's right. She'd stopped taking the Risperdal.'

'Do you know why?'

'Your guess is as good as mine,' he said, sighing.

The two men, lost in their thoughts, looked at each other sidelong, like customers elbow-to-elbow at a shop counter. Only the angle of their shoulders revealed the strain particular to those eaten up by remorse.

Martin accompanied the old man back to his car, an

olive-green vintage Mercedes with cream leather seats. The rain had stopped. A ray of sunlight transformed the puddled tarmac into a mirror. The doctor was looking for his keys, well versed in the exercise after years.

'I'm incapable of always putting them in the same place ... I hope they didn't fall out of my pocket ... '

Martin smiled. He offered to have a look under the car. The doctor put a hand on his arm.

'Don't bother, Martin. Look.'

Through the tinted window, you could make out the keys on the driver's seat. The old man opened the door and picked up the bunch of keys with a little laugh.

'Whatever you do, don't say anything to my wife,' he joked.

'Promise.'

They shook hands warmly. The doctor was about to get into the Mercedes when he thought better of it, throwing the keys back into his palm.

'Martin?'

'Yes?'

'The keys got me thinking ... A police officer questioned me last week about your mother. It seems that she changed the locks.'

'Indeed.'

'So you don't have keys to get into her house any more.'

'No.'

'That's odd.'

'Why?'

'She must have thought that you were up to something.'

Martin shrugged. 'She knew I was going to put her back on her medication.'

'I don't doubt it. But keys are very symbolic. By preventing you from having access to her private life, her world, she's also trying to protect you from it.'

A dozen pigeons crossing the sky caught Martin's eye.

'I hadn't looked at it that way,' he said.

'Do you know by any chance where she kept her notebooks?'

'What notebooks?'

'Elsa wrote down everything she did in little black notebooks the size of a diary.'

Martin had no idea.

'It could be helpful to the police, of course. She had certainly logged a great deal of information in them about her neighbours and the stone boy.'

'The stone boy?'

Dr Mamnoue took his place behind the wheel of his car.

'Yes, that's what she called him, all right. You didn't know?'

The two exchanged contrite looks. The iridescence of

the wet tar disappeared with the arrival of a dark grey cloud.

'Chin up, Martin. I'll see you soon.'

Dr Mamnoue slammed the door three times before it would close. Then he turned the key in the ignition and pulled out of his parking space, leaving Martin standing in a puddle of water.

56

He turned towards her. He could feel her warmth through the sheets. Pressing his stomach against his wife's back, Martin felt desire overwhelm him.

'Martin, I'm sleeping.'

'Morning, love.'

'Not now.'

'I just want to be inside you … just a bit … like that …'

'It's barely seven o'clock.'

'I promise, we won't make love.'

Audrette sighed, then, gradually, once her nightdress was around her waist, she arched her back. She stiffened, grumbled, and let her husband in. Pleasure made its way along the twists and turns of her sleepy body. She pushed back the sheet, Martin threw the duvet to the bottom of the bed with a kick, and they finished in orgasm, almost surprised.

An instant later, Audrette was taking a shower without having kissed her husband, who was supine, stretched out across the mattress.

The night had been short, consumed by a bedtime argument. An exhausting game of unanswered questions, unfeasible plans, built-up frustration, a stream of blame. Audrette longed for a bit of fantasy, a different man than this unshorn, sallow-skinned being that had been haunting the house for ten days, bundled up in a dirty, worn tracksuit, nails bitten to the quick. She was hoping for a dinner in Paris, two tickets to the opera, a drink with friends, to enjoy scallops and tagliatelle in a truffle sauce with old wine; she demanded some kind of lightness, even a little superficiality, a fucking bunch of flowers without the pretext of a celebration, a useless piece of jewellery, a bloody hair clip, a toilet deodoriser wrapped up in tissue paper. She turned back around and hit the pillow with her fist, trying in vain to give it the shape she wanted.

'What do you want, Martin? What are you really looking for at the end of the day?'

Martin wanted nothing like all that. Old wine gave him a headache, friends hadn't been on the agenda for ages, his mother was dying – what was he going to do at the opera, surrounded by old money and bourgeois gits with bad facelifts?

'Right. So that's what culture means to you …'

'I'm tired, Audrette.'

'Unless you want to fuck.'

'You're complaining?'

'You're an asshole.'

'That's it.'

'Bastard.'

'Bitch.'

At about eight o'clock, they made breakfast in the kitchen, each passing the other what they needed: mug, butter, toast, like two children setting the table to please their parents. On France Info, they were reporting on the launch of the vaccination campaign against swine flu. The vaccine had been the number-one concern of the French, except the dairy farmers, who were too busy setting up roadblocks outside milk processing factories in the western Loire. Martin ate alone, letting his coffee go cold in the cup. Audrette had already gone back to her office on the first floor and had turned on her computer, which was logged into the Agreenium site, the official agronomic and veterinary research organisation that she had put together in her role as a teacher and researcher over the last three years at Agro Paris Tech. Unlike her husband, Audrette was making a good career for herself. Her strength of character protected her against drama, like a life insurance policy inherited at birth. Martin envied his wife, or rather admired her, drawing an unhoped-for power from her. He knew she could do anything. Even renting *La Traviata* on DVD, throwing his tracksuit in the rubbish, shaving him against his will and inviting Jean-Hugues and Marine – with their two children – over for a raclette party, all at the same time.

He regretted having called her a bitch.

But she'd deserved it.

He threw the rest of the cold coffee down the sink. He was about to go up for a shower when the doorbell rang.

'Martin, are you expecting someone?' Audrette's voice came down the stairs.

He responded in the negative. Registered post? A gardener? A pain-in-the-arse estate agent? Martin went to the front door and picked up the entry phone. A bluish image appeared on the screen. He recognised the man standing outside his gate immediately.

'Dr Préau?'

'Good morning, Lieutenant.'

'Morning!'

He could see Sevran's breath. The outside temperature on the screen read two degrees.

'Your mobile is going straight to voicemail! Sorry to bother you, but I must speak with you.'

Martin knew he'd be late going into his surgery. And for the first time in his life, he was going to have a cup of coffee with a policeman while wearing his slippers.

57

'Let me get the sugar.'

Audrette's perfume smelled good, with a hint of vanilla. She went from the living room to the kitchen wearing jeans and a jumper, carrying cups and biscuits. The graceful swing of her hips below her belt always had an immediate effect on guests. The lieutenant was no exception to the rule. With his leather aviator jacket, woollen hat and an orange scarf tied under his neck, sitting on the edge of his seat on the white sofa, he looked like the Grinch discovering Snow White.

'Thank you very much, madam.'

He turned to Martin, his eyes keen.

'What does she do for a living, your wife?'

'Modelling.'

'Oh, really?'

'She's an agricultural engineer, actually.'

'Ah.'

Audrette came back with the sugar bowl.

'Is that all right for you, Inspector?'

'Uh, yes, thank you ... Not inspector – lieutenant, madam.'

'Sorry!'

Audrette slipped out of the room, and the lieutenant took off his hat and scarf. The moment had come to move on to more serious matters. He threw a sugar cube into his coffee and stirred it with a little spoon.

'So, we went ahead with a search of your mother's house yesterday morning.'

He put down the spoon, leaned over for his coffee, took a sip, and put it back on the coffee table. Too hot.

'Doctor, if you could rate your mother's mental instability between one and ten, what would you say?'

His legs and arms crossed on the sofa, Martin raised his eyebrows, perplexed.

'I'm a GP, not an expert psychiatrist.'

'I know. OK, let me be clearer.' The officer rooted around inside his jacket and took out an iPhone, which he showed Martin with a hint of malice. 'This is the record of the search. I have all of it in there.'

He pulled a pair of glasses from the other pocket with

a dramatic gesture, and then shook them open sharply and slid them over his ears.

'So, naturally, we found the boxes from the sleeping tablets that were used to poison the madeleines, the tart and the cider. They were empty, in the kitchen bin.' His fingers skimmed over the screen of the telephone, which reflected in his glasses.

'But we also discovered other, more surprising things . . .'

The two phone sockets in the house had been carefully wrapped in aluminium foil. One of the kitchen cupboards had been filled with fifty or so jam jars containing small dusty pebbles. Each jar was labelled, sorted by the week they were collected. In the lieutenant's opinion, this unusual collection confirmed the claims made by the housekeeper and the psychoanalyst regarding the stress on the victim of the building work going on in the neighbourhood. The refrigerator was similarly stocked with jars, but with different contents: kohlrabi, carrots, potatoes, beetroot, radishes, celeriac, root vegetables of all kinds fermenting in brine. The crisper held other surprises: a baffling deflated ball stuffed with soil, along with another jar, both wrapped in plastic bags.

'A jar of pebbles covered in dried blood,' specified the officer.

This unusual jar confirmed for the second time the

housekeeper's statement, in which she had spoken of there being red gravel on one of the windowsills, gravel that the lieutenant had sent off for analysis.

'She was following a strange diet, your mum,' he joked.

Martin didn't react. His left foot bobbed nervously at the end of his leg.

'On the first and second floors, we noticed that all the plumbing – the sink, shower, bidet – were blocked up with corks and reinforced with old rags. So your mother must have been washing herself in basins of water, which she was then emptying down the toilets.'

Sevran straightened his glasses and continued. 'We unblocked them. The smell that came out of the pipes was rotten. We had to break the padlocks on the bathroom window to be able to breathe. I was there – it stank. Is there a problem with the septic tank, Doctor? Has your mother had it emptied recently?'

Martin was evasive in his answer. He had also noticed the bad small that sometimes overwhelmed the house without really knowing the reason for it.

'It's possible that some vermin died in it ... Anyway. In your mother's room, we found a pair of binoculars; she was using them no doubt to spy on the neighbours. In the drawer of the little inlaid table, there were several completely blurry photos – taken from the window there – that were unusable. We also noticed quite a few small bits of dried fruit on the carpet ... Ah! Let's get to the bed: under the blankets, we came upon a big bar of soap.'

'That's one of my grandmother's things. It's supposed to help with the circulation in your legs.'

'Oh. Does it work?'

'If you believe it does, yes.'

'How about a roll's worth of aluminium foil spread out under the mattress; is that one of your grandmother's home remedies, too? Does it cure corns on your feet, maybe?'

Martin sighed. He had spent hours next to that bed. How had he not seen anything?

'Right, I'll carry on . . . On the second-storey landing, we counted ninety mousetraps, a sorry sight: hardened Gruyère rinds everywhere and not one single catch.'

'My mother had been hearing noises in her attic.'

'That's just it, Doctor,' chuckled the bespectacled lieutenant. 'Was it really mice that your mother was hearing?'

'I don't know. It's an old house. Like all old homes, it settles, the pipes make noise—'

'I agree with you, but that isn't what your mother thought. Guess what we found in the utility room, and again in the different rooms in the basement? Twice as many mousetraps. One hundred and ninety-four, to be exact. Why a hundred and ninety-four and not two hundred?'

'The hardware shop had sold out.'

'You could get a job in the police, you could.'

'I'd rather chase germs.'

The officer coughed into his fist, smiling.

'So, we've got one hundred and ninety-four mouse traps, and guess what, Doctor?'

'Not a single dead mouse.'

The lieutenant raised his eyebrows, pleased.

'In fact, there were. But dead ones like these, Doctor, you don't see every day. Our two crime scene colleagues can't get over it.'

Martin uncrossed his legs and put his slippers flat on the floor, trying to channel the stress that the officer was putting him under. He stared at the man, masking his anxiety with a smile.

'Had my mother been collecting something other than stones?'

Lieutenant Sevran took off his glasses and goggled at him with his bright blue eyes.

'Bingo! A collection worthy of the compressions of César![1]'

He turned his mobile around to Martin and showed him three photographs: Martin recognised the freezer in

---

1 French sculptor César (César Baldaccini, 1921–1988) was a founder of the Nouveaux Réalistes group: artists who took inspiration from urban, everyday life and materials. In the early 1960s, César used scrap metal and car parts to mould his works, compressing them to the point of being unrecognisable.

314

the utility room, and what looked like shrivelled animal skins.

'What is that?'

'Cats. Cats that had been put through the wash.'

Martin looked at the snapshots more closely: their fur looked like salt cod.

'My mother did that?'

'Oh, your mother was washing more than just her whites.'

Sevran couldn't hold back a snigger.

'Sorry. Moving along. So, in the middle of all the flattened moggies, we also spotted that.'

With a pointed gesture, Sevran lightly touched the screen of his phone and pulled up another photo.

'The remains of a mobile phone, victim of a ninety-degree eco whites cycle, having been previously smashed to smithereens with a hammer. A Nokia.'

'Shit!' blurted Martin. 'My phone . . .'

'That's what we call a total bug sweep.'

The lieutenant burst into laughter and closed down the window on his electronic toy with his thumb. Martin froze. His mother must be the laughing stock of the whole station. She'll be a poster girl for washing powders! Elsa Préau says 'washing machines live longer with Calgon'! Sevran put the warm iPhone back in his jacket and reached over to try his coffee. It was just right.

'So, Doctor, let me ask you again: if you had to rate

your mother's mental instability from one to ten, what would you give her?'

Martin wiped a limp hand over his face and felt the rasp of his beard.

'A hundred and ninety-four?'

'Seriously.'

'What do you want me to say? That my mother's nuts? Lock her up? People like her with an underlying mental condition and no treatment don't get better, and France has hundreds of thousands of them! Do you think that the capacity of psychiatric hospitals in this country can be increased? Can you imagine how much it would cost our society to feed, care for and process hundreds of thousands of patients? You think what, in the police, that the mentally ill are all psychopaths? That by throwing people practically naked into rooms with no furniture or windows and feeding them meds, that they might somehow have a chance of being cured?'

'Don't get worked up, Doctor.'

Then something unusual happened: someone rang the bell for the second time, and it was only nine o'clock.

'One of your colleagues?' Martin asked.

'I came alone.'

'Don't bother, Martin, I'll get it!' Audrette shouted down the stairs.

She put on a jacket and went out. Martin took the opportunity of the break to go to the toilet. He was fuming. How many times had he heard that? That his mother should be in a straitjacket? 'A tea party turned massacre' the headlines would read in the 'other news' column in the papers. *Paris Match* had rereleased images dating back to the time of the trial, and *Detective* was making it their cover story. Several journalists and two law firms in Paris had already tried to contact Martin at his office. Fortunately the ICU enforced truly draconian visiting policies when it came to accessing his mother's room – otherwise Elsa Préau would already be naked on the Internet. The media technology was clearly superior to that used during the trial. How soon before an iPhone app and SMS voting can decide whether or not Mrs Préau should live or die?

And so the *danse macabre* began again.

Martin lifted the lid of the toilet and relieved himself.

58

Audrette returned a minute later.

'A Christmas present from my parents,' she said, walking across the living room and kissing her husband on the cheek before he sat back down on the couch.

She disappeared into her office with the package under her arm, leaving a scent of vanilla in her wake. Still on the edge of his seat, the police officer waited, almost smiling.

'Do you have other questions to ask me?' asked Martin darkly.

'One or two, Doctor, don't you worry. I was a bit clumsy just now ...'

'Nothing I haven't seen before.'

'What I wanted to tell you, actually, was that with

regards to the search, knowing that your mother had purposely put the sleeping pills in the cakes, knowing, according to Mr Desmoulins' testimony, that she was not of sound mind at the time of the assault, and taking into account the fact that she had stopped taking her medication, it's hard to imagine that this story about the abused kid is true. Rather, it would be all the more reason to suspect – to quote Dr Mamnoue from memory – a hallucination linked to her mental illness. Do you know what that means?'

'But the ball in the fridge, the bloody stones . . . you'd have to take samples, analyse and compare the DNA with the guy my mother suspects of having beaten the kid and who then literally butchered her!'

'Mr Desmoulins defended himself. He defended his family.'

'You can't say that! Did you see the state my mother was in?'

'In an assault, appearances are often deceiving.'

'But . . . what about the little girl's drawing?'

'For us, the investigation stops here, Doctor.'

Martin felt his stomach heave. He was as sick as a dog.

'You can't do that! There's the photo my mother talked about. Did you ever find it? And what about her notebooks? It seems that she wrote everything down in notebooks. She hid them somewhere in the house . . . You have to go back to her place and look for them!'

'That's up to the prosecutor to decide. You seem to forget, Doctor, that whatever her motivations, your mother attempted to commit a crime. And it isn't the first time.'

Martin stood up and took a few steps towards the bay window. Frost hemmed the yellow leaves on the trees in the garden. He ran a hand over his stomach to calm the nervous spasms. Everyone was accusing his mother. Poisoning, assault with her own hammer, irrefutable evidence of premeditation. The report from the search pointed in the direction of a confused mental state. This time, Mrs Préau wouldn't escape a chemical straitjacket; they would destroy her brain cells and turn her into a vegetable.

'The prosecution is going to have trouble putting my mother on the stand,' Martin quipped.

'That's what he'll set about doing if she ever opens her eyes.'

'And if she doesn't?'

Sevran stood too, making his knees crack.

'Mr Desmoulins will probably be investigated for involuntary manslaughter of a vulnerable person.'

So Martin wished the best for his mother: 'Ah, well. Let's hope she dies.'

59

The day that Mrs Préau died was a magnificent November day. The red and gold leaves blazoned in the town. The sun warmed the façades of the greying buildings on Rue Jean Jaurès, and Audrette filled bags with dead leaves on the garden path. She did not expect to see Martin turn up in front of her in the middle of the afternoon, bag in hand, like a student expelled from school, eyes bloodshot. She took off her gardening gloves and went up to him, her muddy rubber boots weighing down her steps. Martin noticed that her nose and cheeks were pearly pink in the sunlight, and that the old and threadbare jumper she wore to work in the garden was too wide for her; it had belonged to him when he was still in medical school. She had appropriated it the first day they made love, slipping it over her bare skin to cross his room and go to the toilet on the landing. Martin had coveted that jumper back then.

'You're home early,' Audrette said softly, hugging her husband.

Martin didn't have the courage to say the words. The man just dropped his bag and squeezed his wife in his arms. They stayed like that until they went numb.

By nightfall, Mr Philippe Desmoulins had been taken into custody and presented to the prosecution. He was being investigated for the involuntary manslaughter of a vulnerable person, taken before the judge, released on bail and required to appear at the police station once a week for the duration of the trial.

SEEING IS BELIEVING

'But tomorrow! Terrible tomorrow!
When your weakened organs, the
nerves worn thin, the titillating
yearning to cry, the impossibility of
applying yourself to any work tell
you that you have played a forbidden
game. Hideous nature, stripped of
last night's glow, resembles the
melancholy debris of a celebration.'

Charles Baudelaire, 'Moral',
Artificial Paradises

60

'Hello?'

'Hello, this is ChildLine. I'm listening . . . '

'A lady told me I could call this number . . . '

'Yes, hello. I'm listening to you.'

'She gives me piano lessons. She told me that this was a secret number and that she knew it because she was a teacher before. But it's not a secret number.'

'No. It's a number you must have seen on a poster in your school.'

'Yes.'

'Do you know why children ring this number?'

'Yes. When someone's hurting them.'

'What's your name?'

' . . . My name is Laurie.'

'Hello, Laurie. Could you tell me how old you are?'

'I'm seven years old.'

'My name's Odile and I'm here to help you. Now that we know each other's names, can you tell me why you called?'

'For Kévin.'

'Who is Kévin?'

'My little brother.'

'Are you worried about your little brother?'

'Yes. Because of my dad.'

'Your daddy isn't nice to your brother?'

'No.'

'Does he hurt him?'

' . . . I wouldn't want Kévin to go down into the basement.'

'Why are you afraid of your brother going into the basement?'

' . . . '

'Laurie, has your dad been violent towards you?'

'No, not with me, with my other brother . . . I hafta hang up, my granny has come home . . . '

'Laurie, can you tell me where you're calling us from?'

'From my granny's house.'

'What town does your granny live in?'

'In Auxerre.'

'And you, what town do you live in?'

'I can't tell you . . . I have to go . . . '

'Laurie. . . Hello?'

61

The death of Mrs Préau had two notable effects on her son. He stopped biting his nails, and he started to lose his hair. Audrette's grief manifested itself differently. Three weeks after her mother-in-law's funeral, she became pregnant.

The couple were euphoric for a short while – a month and a half. Before the miscarriage. But the hope of an unborn baby had well and truly taken hold. Martin's wife was determined. She fell pregnant in the next six weeks and gained weight quickly, as if she were fortifying the walls of a castle. This time, life stuck.

The press had shown surprising discretion with respect to Martin. When the evil grandmother left the stage, leaving the audience with a dry trial, the media hype dropped off completely, the journalists in a sulk. Martin mourned unthinkingly, working through the administrative details of his mother's death, filling out forms, shaking unknown hands. At the reading of the will, which had been written before 1997, he wasn't at all surprised to learn that his mother had bequeathed her house to Bastien. However, a clause stipulated that in case of the death of the heir, the property valued at €700,000 would go to a charity dedicated to child protection, provided that the latter resell it to *a couple with children*. Martin inherited everything else. A hundred thousand euros in various savings accounts, and furniture, which he quickly divested himself of by contacting Emmaus. Martin only kept a few family heirlooms and the small inlaid table he had given his mother for her last birthday. To this was added thirty boxes filled with personal effects: memories of thousands of students in plastic bags, and various personal and other letters, photographs, collections of old postcards. Finally, Martin's father had not been forgotten: he received the Gaveau 'in memory of wonderful childhood memories shared around Erik Satie'. The instrument was the weight of ten dead donkeys. It would be difficult to slide it into a FedEx package to Montreal.

'The bitch!' was Audrette's only comment on the misadventure of the disinherited son.

At his surgery, Dr Préau's patients did not fail to offer their condolences – with or without an ulterior motive.

Some, those with a parent suffering from mental illness, shared his grief sincerely. The few hateful anonymous letters that he received in the weeks following the attack at the Desmoulins family home had dried up.

When he was coming home at night, lowering the car window to breathe in the fragrances spilling out of the gardens of suburban houses on the edge of town, aromas of roses, laburnum and lilac, and wafts of shish kebabs and merguez, Dr Préau allowed himself to have some hope. If he left the task of organising the house in anticipation of its new resident to Audrette, unable to project himself into the near future, he willingly indulged ironing – a static activity Audrette discouraged. Since the age of six, Martin had acquired a true mastery of this skill, thus easily earning his pocket money. He knew how to do the basics, set the table, hoover and dust, and many other household chores shared willy-nilly with his mother. She had been preparing him constantly for his future role as a husband – or as the perfect bachelor. Once the clothes were folded and put away in the wardrobe, Martin ran aground on the sofa against his wife, one hand on her little round stomach, and slept for about twenty-two hours, sated with tenderness.

In a year or two, the trial would take place; he would be called to testify, as would Dr Mamnoue, and he would try to rehabilitate the memory of his mother, in vain. Dead Elsa Préau was no longer of interest to anyone.

62

He had forgotten the beauty mark. Discrete, below the left cheek, and that gently parted mouth, as if a regret might escape from it, a sweet nothing, a silly comment. She was there, a few metres away from him, sitting in the waiting room, her coat on her knees, alone. Some ten years had passed. Martin remembered when and how he had made love to this woman. Forcefully, three times, almost bloody-mindedly. Why her and not the others? She wasn't even the first of a series of romantic dalliances. Curled up on a chair, she seemed smaller and more severe.

Maybe it was the boots and polo neck? And him? What was he like in his wide-wale velvet jacket and Timberlands?

'Valérie?'

A lock of hair fell into her face. She pushed it aside, staring at the man who stood in the hallway, bag in hand.

'Hello, Doctor.'

She smiled. It was half past two, Martin was returning from his lunch break. With a gesture, he invited her to follow him into his office. Rising, she unfolded the body he had enjoyed, and which still made an impression on him. Her figure had gained in years, curves and abundance. He hurried to close the door behind her.

'Valérie Tremblay . . . The last I heard about you was at a police station.'

'I'm still working there.'

They exchanged a friendly kiss.

'How are you? What are you up to? Do have a seat.'

After a brief exchange about their lives, in which each pretended to have found a good balance, Valérie explained why she was there, which owed nothing to chance. The social worker hadn't come to choose a new referring physician, either. And what she had to say would get Martin into an entirely different kind of trouble.

'Before telling you why I'm here, I wanted to tell you how saddened I was by your mother's death and how much I regret not having had the courage to come to see you sooner.'

She crossed her legs. She winced slightly. She must

have a bad back – or what she had to say weighed heavily on her heart.

'I can't say that I knew your mother well – I only saw her once. But I can't get it out of my mind that I was partly responsible for her death.'

Martin came back down to earth with a thud. He was looking at an alien. No one had ever expressed such feelings towards his mother.

'You know that she had made an official report for the police logbook. After her statement, I contacted her so that we could meet.'

'The police lieutenant filled me in. She brought you a photo of an abused child, is that right?'

'I saw her on Monday, the twenty-sixth of October, five days before the attack. And I called her back on Thursday to tell her that I couldn't do anything, because aside from her report, there was no evidence that a child of the age she described was in close contact with the neighbours. That's when she told me about the photo.'

'But no one ever saw that photo.'

'No. But I know that it exists.'

'Really?'

'Last week, Sevran contacted the photo labs in town.'

'Sevran has reopened the investigation?'

'A man confirmed having printed the blurry pictures found at your mother's during the search. But he also remembered having made enlargements of another photo that wasn't among them – one of the face of a little boy with dark curly hair, aged about seven or eight.'

'Why did the police reopen the case?'

'Because something happened at the Desmoulins' house.'

Valérie lowered her eyes, embarrassed.

'Could we go outside somewhere to talk about it? A café?'

The bistro in the market square wasn't at all welcoming. On this rainy October day, the windows were steamed up, and nothing could have warmed the fake leather banquettes. Sitting in the back of the room by the bay window, they drank coffees sticky as pitch. With her coat hanging over her shoulders, Valérie brought her face close to Martin's.

'Ordinarily, I would never have the right to bring up ongoing cases, but because I know you and because I feel partially responsible, I wanted to speak to you about it before Sevran called you. He's a good policeman. He's very good at his job. And I very much like working with him. But I think that this time he was backing the wrong horse.'

'Valérie, tell me what you know.'

She sat up straight and placed her palms on the Formica table.

'Philippe Desmoulins was charged with involuntary manslaughter and was released on police bail until the trial. But at his lawyer's request, the condition that he appear at the police station was dropped after seven months by the judge. The Desmoulins sold the house and left the area.'

'Where did they go?'

'We don't know.'

'What do you mean?'

'The address that they gave their lawyer was fake.'

Martin ran a hand through his hair. He gave himself an odd cowlick at the top of his head.

'Shit! Was my mother right? Was that bastard hitting his kid?'

'That's not all. The new owners moved in in August. Two weeks ago, they had water damage in the house. They had to redo the floor in the kitchen, and they got some contractors in. The workers started by pulling up the floating floorboards. And there, inside a broom cupboard, they found a trapdoor. A locked trapdoor.'

Martin slumped on the banquette.

'Could the police have missed it?'

'Martin, no one ever believed that a child existed. The police forensic team didn't see anything because they didn't look. The guys from the lab examined the back of the cupboard where your mother had hit. They testified that there were breezeblocks behind the wooden panelling, and that was the end of it. They didn't probe the floor. In the crime scene photos—'

'You saw them?'

'Sevran showed me a few bits of the file. We're very friendly,' she added, blushing. 'In one of the shots, you can see lots of stuff crammed down into the bottom of the cupboard: household cleaners, basins, sponges, a shovel, a broom ... The kind of mess that nobody would think of removing to see what was underneath.'

Martin took a deep breath and made a sign to the barman.

'Go ahead, Valérie.'

'The new owners are from Paris. A young couple with two children. They didn't know about the tragedy that took place in their house. Can you imagine? I wouldn't want to be the agent who sold them the house ... But the contractors, they knew, and they thought it was better to contact the police before touching the trapdoor.'

Martin raised his hand higher.

'Excuse me! A brandy.'

'Two!' Valérie corrected him.

The barman called back the order from the bar. Valérie continued with her story on fast-forward: 'So Sevran rolls up and has the trapdoor opened. It gives onto a windowless room with a low ceiling that must have originally been a storeroom. On the ground they found a mattress, half-burnt and bloodstained, along with an iron bar ... They took loads of swabs ... '

Martin had both elbows on the table and covered his mouth with his fists.

'The kid was there.'

'Sevran isn't so sure of that,' said Valérie flatly.

The barman brought over the little glasses of alcohol. They emptied them in a few gulps. Martin put Valérie's coat back on her shoulders.

'Martin, when your mother came to see me, I believed her. Without a shadow of a doubt. She trusted me. And then, after she assaulted her neighbours, I learned from my colleagues what she had done to your son. So I thought that she had imagined the mistreated child. Like everyone else. Even though I wanted to believe her story.'

'You did your job. You couldn't do anything else.'

'We don't even know who the boy is ... God knows where he is now, what he's going through ... '

She looked down at her handbag, searching for a tissue.

'Sorry. I never cry, shit ... Tears never helped anyone.'

Martin gently caressed her cheek.

'This time they did.'

63

At three o'clock, a retired couple and two African mothers with their babies were sitting in the waiting room. Martin gave himself ten minutes to call Audrette and filled her in on his meeting with the social worker. He promised to come home as soon as possible, but wasn't able to leave the surgery until seven forty-five. When he arrived back home, he was surprised that Audrette hadn't thought to turn on the garden lights outside. There weren't lights on inside the house, either. The table wasn't set, and there was nothing simmering in the kitchen.

'Audrette? You home?'

Martin turned on the light. Audrette was sitting on the sofa, stock still, her round belly visible.

'What's wrong?' Martin asked, worried. 'What are you doing in the dark?'

He knelt down beside her and took her hands in his.

'Are you not feeling well? Your hands are burning up . . . Is it the baby? Are you having contractions?'

'No.'

Martin put a hand on her forehead, then grasped her left wrist to check her pulse. Audrette pulled back her arm.

'I'm fine, Martin, it's not that.'

He stood back up. There were dark circles under her eyes and her face was drawn. She looked overwrought.

'Did something happen to your parents?' he asked, sitting at her side.

She shook her head, staring at her belly.

'Darling, you're worrying me, tell me what's happened.'

'Earlier, when you phoned, you spoke about the child that your mother might have seen in the neighbours' garden, who looked like Bastien.'

'Yes?'

'You said it might not have been her crazy imagination.'

'It's more than likely,' he said, putting an arm around his wife's shoulders.

'I know where the photo is that the police are looking for.'

Martin asked Audrette to repeat what she had just said.

'Do you remember the day that the policeman came to the house to say that he was closing the case?'

'Yes.'

'A package came in the post.'

'A package from your parents, for Christmas.'

Audrette didn't answer. Her husband blinked.

' . . . My mother? Mum sent me something?'

'I don't know what came over me. I couldn't deal with your mother any more. She was destroying our lives, she was destroying you. The package that she had addressed to you, it was . . . I didn't want her to hurt you any more. I tore open a corner of the package, and I saw these photos . . . '

She lifted her right hand gently. Audrette was holding two photographs that her belly was hiding from Martin. One was an enlargement of the other. He seized the enlargement and scrutinised the blurry contours of the child's face. Black curly hair, cheeks pale and hollow.

'Good Lord!'

'He looks so much like Bastien . . . '

Martin stopped himself from retching. He put the enlargement down on the coffee table and got up, not knowing what to do with his hands.

'Where were the photos?'

'In a drawer in my office,' she murmured. 'For almost a year.'

'What else was there in the package?'

'Notebooks. Five notebooks.'

'What did you do with them?'

'They're here, in the house.'

Martin stamped his feet.

'Well, there's a stroke of luck, you didn't throw them out.'

'Removing them, yes; destroying them, no. Your mother would have come back from the dead to punish me,' she joked.

'Stop talking rubbish. Did you read them?'

'I didn't open them. I couldn't bear the thought of reading horrible things about our son, you or me.'

Martin tried to remain calm by pacing the length and breadth of the room.

'An investigation was underway, my mother was between life and death, a life that she had just risked to save the life of a kid, and you didn't even wonder if those photos and notebooks might have been of some importance?'

'I wanted to protect you, Martin. You weren't at all well.'

He glared at Audrette, took three steps towards the bay window and pressed his forehead against it.

'I did it for your own good, I promise you.'

The contact with the frozen glass surprised him. Outside in the shadowy garden, the bluish spectre of a cedar tree loomed.

'Tell me where the notebooks are.'

'I put them in your office.'

Martin snatched up the photos. Audrette snapped out of it. She held her belly, looking guilty.

'I didn't want ... I'm sorry ... '

'Not as sorry as I am!' he shouted, leaving the room.

Audrette ate alone at about nine o'clock. She took her husband a glass of wine and sandwiches on sliced bread. At ten, she went back to get the plate and empty glass, and quietly wished him goodnight.

Martin, absorbed in his reading, didn't respond.

64

Each notebook was about a specific period. The oldest went back to January 1997, six months before Elsa Préau decided to put an end to her days and those of her grandson. The moleskin cover was faded and the pages dog-eared here and there. Martin didn't open it right away. He was wary of that whole period and dreaded reading what Audrette termed 'horrible things', preferring to get into the more recent ones.

Three notebooks had been written in the rest home that Dr Mamnoue had recommended to her, in Hyères, where she had spent the last ten years. She consigned her dreams to it, the dinners that she cooked in her kitchenette, the annoying habits of her neighbours whose moans and snores could be heard through the partition walls, observations of numerous birds frequenting the residence's park, summaries of her reading ... Many repeated the same words that she had used in her letters to her son twice a month. Martin noticed a considerable number of notes based on the archives and documents from the historical society of the town of his birth: there was a commentary on a document dating from 1614, going back to the first parish registry. Did his mother send herself photocopies of the documents by post? By all appearances, she had begun genealogical research into her ancestors. One note had been dedicated to Philippe Angélique de Froissy, who in 1718 married François Henri, the Count of Ségur, forebear of Sophie Rostopchine, Countess of Ségur. Was Elsa Préau related to a grand dame of children's literature, or was it pure fantasy? As he flipped through the pages, Martin slipped into the private life of a mother whose mind wandered into a thousand things, commenting on the scandal of agricultural prices dropping for farmers and improving as man-made air pollution increased. Pages in which she discussed her memories were rare. Only one had to do with his maternal grandmother, Deborah, when she took Elsa as a child to walk along the Marne on Sunday.

There was one notebook left, filled with a nervous handwriting, in which the notes went back to July 2009, so four months before her death. It was about two in the morning when Martin began reading it.

It was all there.

Him.

Audrette.

The Desmoulins.

And the stone boy.

At about five o'clock, Audrette was woken by a contraction. She turned over to change position and discovered her husband sitting in the armchair next to the bed. He was holding the oldest notebook open in front of him. Inside it was a retro postcard of the old town train station, which he was using as a bookmark; the reverse bore the inscription, *For my unbelieving son, take care.*

'Martin . . .'

He ran a hand through his dishevelled hair and coughed.

'I knew that it would hurt you to read those notebooks . . . Come to bed. It's very late.'

Martin pulled himself up with difficulty and held up the notebook to his wife.

'You have to read that.'

'But, darling . . .'

'Do you remember what she said about you in court?' he growled in a broken voice. 'That you "carried evil in you" but that she forgave you because you didn't know, or something like that?'

'Does she talk about it in her journal?'

'They're notes that she took somewhere from a

medical text. They go back to April nineteen ninety-seven.'

Audrette obeyed. She put two pillows behind her back, lifted her belly, placed the moleskin notebook on it and read:

For the majority of people diagnosed with leukaemia, there is no way to determine its cause. In some cases, particular risk factors can be singled out:

accidental exposure to radioactivity,

exposure in utero to X-rays,

exposure to certain chemicals (benzene, hydrocarbon fumes) or to certain fertilisers,

exposure (including in utero or low-dose) to certain pesticides.

According to a metastudy performed on 31 epidemiological studies done between 1950 and 2009, maternal exposure through her work during pregnancy doubled the risk of leukaemia in the child (an increase of 40 per cent in farmers, who seemed to be most exposed). This risk of childhood leukaemia increases in cases of exposure to insecticide and herbicide (+ 2.7 and 3.7, respectively).

The last paragraph was underlined with a continuous line.

Audrette closed the notebook.

She put her hands on her belly.

As an agricultural engineer, herbicides had been the major focus of her studies at the time.

'She knew about Bastien,' Martin murmured. 'She even knew why he had contracted that disease.'

Audrette made a face and calmed her false contraction with a breathing exercise.

65

The enlargement given by Martin to Lieutenant Sevran was entered into the missing persons file. The picture would be put up in police stations; the stone boy would join Estelle Mouzin.[2] The media in turn were quick to publish the photograph. Forty-eight hours later, the little boy was recognised by a teacher working in Auxerre, Ms Le Buisson. The prosecutor handed the matter over to the juvenile crimes division.

---

2 Estelle Mouzin was nine years old when she disappeared on 9 January 2003 in Guermantes, Seine-et-Marne on her way home from school. Though her case was covered extensively in the French press, and reopened repeatedly by the police as they followed different domestic and international lines of inquiry, she has never been found.

At six months' pregnant, Audrette had gained 10 kilos and was wearing it so well that it was difficult for her husband to prevent her from running to the hardware shop where she pushed trolleys loaded down with pots of paint, wallpaper borders, fairy lights, curtains and flat-pack furniture for the baby's room. Martin left her to it, stunned by the energy exuded by this pregnant woman with the appetite of a lumberjack. She was capable of spending three hours sitting on the couch comparing and matching up colours – an exercise that her husband would have finished off in two minutes. Audrette's growth was translating into a daily need for sexual gratification. Martin didn't know quite how to take this, perturbed by this unknown person that she was carrying, whose sex they now knew. He was disoriented by his wife's changing body, yes, but the prospect of rediscovering his role as a father was scarier by far. Had he not failed the first time, unable to protect his son from disease and death? Martin redoubled his efforts at work. He did extra house calls, eating sandwiches in his car for lunch. He would come home so exhausted that Audrette had no choice but to tuck her husband up in bed, knowing well what effect frustration had on her man.

Then one morning he received an urgent call from the police. Sevran had news.

'This case is still going to be run by social services,' he said, coming to meet him in the lobby.

Martin followed him to his office on the first floor. At nine o'clock, 13 rue Parmentier was brimming with activity. Policemen and women grazed past each other in the narrow hallway, staring at Martin as they passed. Sevran's office was unusually tidy: the pens were tucked into a pencil holder, his files were lined up on the shelf and the mouse pad had been changed – the new one was bright yellow, with a smiley face. The lieutenant had swapped his jacquard jumper for a black and grey striped polo neck. In one year, something had changed. There was probably a woman in his life. And Martin guessed her name.

'I understand that our social worker contacted you recently.'

'Indeed. Valérie Tremblay came to see me at my office.'

'Anything she might have told you about the inquiry is strictly confidential.'

'Of course.'

'Good.'

The lieutenant paused and began again in a clear voice: 'Rémi Chaumoi. The child who your mother saw in her neighbours' garden is called Rémi Chaumoi.'

Martin closed his eyes.

'Are you all right, Doctor? Because I've only just begun.'

She hadn't been wrong. His mother was never wrong.

The stone boy had been real. Martin's heart, swollen with guilt, leapt in his chest. He opened his eyes.

'I'm very well, Lieutenant. Go ahead.'

Sevran recounted what he knew of the story. Rémi Chaumoi had been the pupil of Ms Le Buisson, from 2004 to 2006. She remembered him clearly. The child had behavioural difficulties. Particularly in his last year. He had become aggressive and reacted badly to authority. Ms Le Buisson had once witnessed his being hysterical when his mother dropped him off at school. When he was asked to take off his coat, he shouted and took all of his clothes off, throwing his things around the classroom. The teacher had calmed him by rocking him in her arms. She had then seen marks on the child's body where he had been struck. The parents were called in by the school's headmaster, and the information had been passed on to social services. The father did not appear at the meeting. The headmaster, Mr Tissey, met the mother along with her older daughter, who was pregnant. He told the police how surreal the meeting had been, as the mother seemed to hold her daughter responsible for the child's strange behaviour. As for the bruising on his body, she maintained that it was the result of his behaviour; he was unruly, and lashed out at everything. The same statement was repeated in front of the social worker at the Chaumoi family meeting at the social welfare centre.

'A year later, the child was no longer going to school.

No one was worried. Except the teacher. Ms Le Buisson got back in contact with the family and learned that the child had been handed over to his older sister, who had just got married and was currently living near Paris. End of story.'

Martin nodded.

'The third child was Mrs Desmoulins' younger brother,' he murmured.

'That's what my colleagues in juvenile crimes thought. Until we went to see Rémi's mother in Auxerre.'

The lieutenant sat down in his armchair and crossed his arms.

'When they stuck the photo under her nose, she recognised her "little Rémi" right away. At first, she denied knowing where her daughter and son-in-law were. So my colleagues got out the photos of the soiled mattress, and let loose about failing to come to the aid of a person in danger. Mrs Chaumoi was afraid that it would come back on her, so she let slip that the Desmoulins were in Belgium. They were hiding in Courtrai. They were arrested three days ago.'

'Were the children with them?'

'The two younger ones, yes. But not Rémi Chaumoi.'

Sevran picked a little wooden ruler out of the pencil pot and used it to scratch his neck.

'That's where we are. Mrs Chaumoi said something else to juvenile crimes.'

He put the ruler back in the pot.

'Rémi wasn't her son, but the son of her daughter, Blandine Desmoulins.'

'What's this, now?'

'Nothing too original. The kind of sordid affair we see often enough: the kid discovers she's up the duff at sixteen, and it's too late for an abortion. Out of shame, for fear of wagging tongues, the family decides to hide the pregnancy. The kid gives birth at her parents' home, and a week later, the child is registered under the grandmother's name.'

'Her first birth, at home, at sixteen? That's medically risky.'

'According to my colleagues, the Chaumoi family isn't exactly made up of Nobel prize-winners in the natural sciences – more like the types to stick on porno flicks in front of the kids. The joint where they were living was something else, apparently. Aside from an enormous country-style kitchen that must have cost them a packet in credit, the rest of the place was revolting. Old carpet in all the rooms and on all the walls, bare wires running along the skirting boards, rooms that were never aired out that smelled to high heaven, and a garden turned into a dump where they were raising rabbits in jerry-rigged supermarket trollies.'

'Rémi grew up there,' Martin muttered.

'A charming nursery! His second one wasn't bad either,' he joked.

'So the child was the victim of mistreatment by his own parents?'

'Point of information . . . ' The officer raised the index finger of his left hand, pointing at the ceiling. 'Desmoulins isn't Rémi's father. We have a test confirming it, comparing his DNA taken at the time of his first arrest at the station with one from the soiled mattress: no relation.'

'So, his step-father was hitting him?'

'Exactly. He couldn't handle the idea that his wife had known another man before him. And it's the kid who got the brunt of it.'

'And Rémi's mother didn't do anything to stop him. He really was a martyred child . . . '

'I need a coffee. You want one?'

'No thanks.'

'Something else? A glass of water? I'll bring you one.'

The lieutenant disappeared from his office in a flash, leaving the door open, as was his habit. Martin looked out of the window at the sky becoming a grey-blue.

Sometimes, what he saw of his patients' private lives wasn't always rosy. Like the young woman who was six months' pregnant, whose husband left her with three children. The father had gone back to Africa because he found Paris 'too cold'. Dr Préau had seen her in the car park at the Intermarché one Saturday afternoon, with her three children and her big belly, a trolley filled with frozen pizzas and fruit juice, desperately waiting for a taxi that wouldn't come. Martin had given the whole family a lift in his car, cramming the food in the boot, and then had driven the young woman home – to newly allocated public housing. She had been left totally to her own devices; she couldn't drive, she had barely enough to feed her children and no one to help her other than her mother, who worked all week.

Martin spent time with her at each of his visits. He told her about her rights and put her in contact with social services. The child was born full term. Then the father returned. And Martin didn't see the young woman in his waiting room again. Until he happened upon her in A&E at Montfermeil one night, her face swollen and one shoulder dislocated.

His ability to block out that kind of experience was indispensable in his job. Too much empathy could kill a doctor, little by little. The world of human misery that Martin navigated contained so much violence and sadism. He tried to help, and often did, but nothing could pretend to protect people from hardship.

'I got you an Evian. It's not the best. I like Luchon better myself. But we can't get a distributor for it.'

Martin took the bottle that was being held out to him along with a clear cup. Sevran took his place back behind his desk, sighing, holding a steaming plastic cup in his hands. He decanted it into his Chupa Chups mug.

'What's troubling us, Doctor, is that this whole thing made us look like fools.'

Martin opened the bottle without looking away from Sevran.

'Yes, but I haven't told you all of it. It'll be in the papers in a few hours. It's probably already on the Internet. We found Rémi Chaumoi. Well, according to the medical examiner, it's very likely that it's him.'

Ice-cold water poured into Martin's cup.

Outside, it was snowing.

66

The child's body was located exactly where Laurie had drawn it, where Elsa Préau saw it appear each Sunday, under the weeping birch, buried a metre or so deep, wrapped in a blanket.

The DNA tests would take a few weeks. But the medical examiner could already provide some information about the general state of the child before his death. The poor condition of Rémi Chaumoi's teeth, the presence of old fractures in his skeleton and the hollow in his skull – the result of a violent blow with a metal bar and his cause of death – spoke of the nutritional deficiencies and abuse that he suffered. If it was difficult to put an exact date on his death, the retrieval of certain evidence steered the technical division towards a hypothesis – a hypothesis that would be confirmed later by Desmoulins before the judge. The presence of minuscule bloodstains on the mattress and the child's clothing (not the result of spatter, but probably from drops from his stepfather's wounded arm) along with a bloody print taken from the door of the cupboard that belonged to Desmoulins (visible in the pictures, but not taken into consideration in the early days of the investigation) allowed them to establish that the child had been killed in the minutes after Mrs Préau fell in the kitchen. Rémi's stepfather caved in his skull 'so that the cops wouldn't hear him screaming', he explained.

One question haunted Martin. Why did this scumbag Desmoulins call the police?

'I've thought about that a lot,' Audrette answered.

Sitting in a wicker armchair in the middle of the baby's room, she was folding lilac baby clothes, which she then put into the drawers of an apple-green dresser.

'What are Philippe Desmoulins' options? His beloved wife and kids are half-conscious. He has one arm in bits and can barely stand. He can't do much other than call for help, even if there's a risk they'll find the kid. Will you pass me those Babygros, please?'

Martin handed his wife the little pile of warm, freshly ironed laundry.

'I understand why Sevran wouldn't be too sure. In this situation, the cops would be careful with a homicide.'

'Did Sevran tell you that Desmoulins had a record?'

'Not enough to make anyone worry – misspent youth stuff, driving under the influence.'

'Huh! That reminds me of someone. A famous twenty-fourth of December, St Adèle's Day.'

'Let me remind you that both of us had been drinking that day.'

'Look! It's started snowing.'

Through the bedroom window, snowflakes danced, pushed by the wind, wheeling towards the tops of the pine trees.

'Adèle … Adélie … That's pretty, Adélie. I like that.'

'You want to name our daughter after part of Antarctica?'

'*En terre Adélie!* Nine hundred thousand kilometres of ice. A heart that's hard to conquer … Adélie would share her saint's day with Adèle. What do you think, love?'

Audrette spoke to her belly as she rubbed it, nearly joyful. Fear of childbirth would come later, with the panic of a contraction far more aggressive than the last. Martin left his wife to her baby talk and walked out of the room.

As he went down to the utility room, the memory of something Dr Mamnoue said about one of his mother's dreams came back to him; the one where a window was 'fighting' with the wind and the curtains were 'angry', and the child – Bastien or Rémi – was playing the piano, his face and mouth stained with dirt. Had she foreseen a terrible fate or expressed her outrage at the death of her grandson, as the psychiatrist thought? His mother had only been wrong about one thing: the stones in the jar. Six months after the assault at the Desmoulins' home, the DNA test results had come back. The blood belonged to an animal. *Felis silvestris catus*. Thus the trail definitively went cold as far as the existence of a child was concerned. Martin plugged in the iron, turned up the temperature to the maximum setting and threw a sheet across the table to iron.

67

Three days before Christmas, Martin received a call in his office. There were fewer patients, so between appointments he was catching up on reading lab leaflets and sorting through old post.

'Am I disturbing you?'

'No, not at all. How are you?'

'Well, thanks. I've just left the police station.'

'Oh yeah?'

Valérie Tremblay's voice was completely flat.

'My job as social worker has been transferred to Clichy-Montfermeil, at the new police station promised by the government after the riots in 2005.'

'You don't seem too enthusiastic about it.'

'I don't know anyone there. I'll lose all my contacts. As

if they couldn't have created a job for me. What will happen to the people who need me here? Who's going to help them? Let's talk about something else.'

The social worker hadn't just called Martin to wish him a happy Christmas. She wanted to know if he had received a letter sent by the juvenile crimes division.

'It's nothing important, don't worry. It's from Laurie Desmoulins.'

Martin put the phone on speaker and picked up the pile of letters that had amassed on his desk. He sifted through them quickly before putting his hand on a brown envelope with the insignia of the French Republic on it.

'I think I have it. How is she?'

'She must be traumatised by her parents' arrest. She's been placed in a foster family and separated from her brother.'

'The poor things.'

Martin rummaged in his desk drawer and found a letter-opener.

'Sevran had got news of her from the juvenile crimes investigators,' Valérie continued. 'She hadn't been very forthcoming with the police. But the drawings that she did at the psychologist's spoke volumes. In one of them, she's drawn herself, holding a telephone. A bubble is coming out of the phone and in it she wrote the number for ChildLine. That allowed juvenile crimes to go back to listen to a call she made last August.'

'Had she called the number?' Martin asked, slicing open the envelope.

'Yes. Her father had become violent with her little brother. Kévin was drawn very small next to her with red tears like fat raindrops. Do you know who told her about that phone number?'

Martin pulled a sheet of paper out of the envelope.

'My mother,' he said, surprised to discover a drawing.

'Yes. The little girl hadn't said enough for them to be able to act at the time. She had totally understood what had happened and why her parents were in prison, even if she preferred to be with them. But she refused to believe that the old lady who gave her piano lessons was dead.'

The drawing, done in coloured pencil, showed a big house with two big eyes. It took up almost the whole page.

'Your mother had promised her something that the little girl hasn't forgotten . . . '

In front of the door, Laurie had drawn her piano teacher, with a smiling face, a helmet of hair on her head, dressed in a long purple dress. She held in her hand an object that Martin didn't recognise right away.

'What was the promise?'

'She would teach her to make crêpes.'

In Elsa Préau's hand, Laurie Desmoulins had drawn a

frying pan. Martin and Valérie wished each other a happy Christmas.

The doctor got a box of drawing pins out of his desk drawer.

He chose four in different colours.

A minute later, the drawing was up on one of the walls of his office.

68

Dr Gérard Préau stroked the walnut-veneer frame. He crouched down to feel the base of the columns of the carved console.

'It really is a marvel,' he murmured admiringly.

He got up, brushed the dust off of his hands and looked at his son, moved.

'Do you know why your mother so wanted me to inherit her Gaveau?'

'The two of you did things on the piano?'

The old man smiled. His steamy breath escaped from his mouth. Martin's garage where the instrument had been stored was never more than six degrees.

'More than that,' he answered. 'Your mother, at the time, had literally enchanted me.'

He lifted the cover and tinkled the keys covered in yellowed ivory. The piano sounded sadly out of tune.

'Elsa fascinated me.'

'Really?'

'Someone who talks to ghosts is by definition captivating.'

Martin pulled up the collar of his jacket.

'Mum was a bit special.'

'She was an exceptional woman.'

'But you left her.'

Dr Gérard Préau met his son's eyes.

'Because she asked me to, Martin. And I think that it's the greatest proof of her love that she ever gave me.'

Martin scraped his heel through the dust, tracing sinuous lines across the tiled floor.

'That, Dad, you'll have to explain.'

Martin's father closed the cover of the piano and put the plastic tarp back in place to protect it from the dust.

'Your mother was a very good mother, and a remarkable teacher. But she would have driven any man in her life mad, starting with me. She had to have it all. We lived in an exhausting meeting of minds. She made of me what she would. When I found myself back in Algeria, I understood just how symbiotic our relationship was, fed by our own frustrations, our childhood suffering, our hopes, our aspirations . . .'

Martin gave a nervous laugh.

'This has to be the first time you've ever spoken about her like that.'

The old man looked annoyed.

'Have I ever said a bad word about her to you?'

'. . . No. That's true.'

'I warned you about her excesses, her contradictions, but never against her. And if mental illness did take such a firm hold on her, it's because pain carved a bottomless pit in her.'

Martin's father took a handkerchief out of one of his pockets and blew his nose discreetly.

'Why didn't you come to the funeral?' Martin asked brusquely.

'She was dead. I didn't see what my presence would have changed. And you seemed perfectly capable of dealing with it by yourself.'

The handkerchief went back in his pocket.

Martin stiffened.

Something wasn't right.

His father had never seemed so upset talking about his mother. In the last weeks since her death, he hadn't stopped making his almost shocking indifference clear to him by phone and email. Up until now, when he got emotional when faced with an old piano no one knew what to do with, himself first and foremost.

'Did Elsa ever speak to you about her mother?' he asked in a broken voice.

'Not much. She died when Mum was very young, right?'

'A bit before the end of the war. Your mother was eight.'

Gérard Préau took a few steps, and shivered.

'Do you know what happened to her?'

Martin repeated what his mother had told him: that his grandmother had left the house one day and never come back, because she had been unhappy with her husband. She had got together with a man somewhere, with whom she made a new life. An adventurer, or a rich business-man.

His father cast his eyes down to the beige buttons on his coat.

'That – that's just the fairy tale she told herself. One day in May nineteen forty-four, my aunt Deborah, Elsa's mother, went to turn herself in to the French police. The idea of not following her parents and her brothers and sisters into deportation had become unbearable to her.'

'What?'

The old man opened the garage door, letting a glacial wind cut inside. He gestured to Martin to follow him.

'She was among the last people deported from the camp at Drancy. She never found her family members. Deborah, née Mathias, was gassed on arrival at Auschwitz. A pointless sacrifice.'

'Why? Why did she do that?' demanded Martin, stupefied, following his father.

'She was Jewish, Martin. Like your mother. And like you.'

Martin needed more than a coffee to warm him up. Standing in the kitchen, his hands still frozen from the December cold, he stared at the contents of the boiling cup between his fingers. His father was busy putting logs in the living-room fireplace. The crackle of the fire highlighted the woolly silence that reigned in the house in the absence of Audrette and Madelyn, Gérard's second wife, who had gone out to pick up useless Christmas nonsense in the Rosny II shopping centre. Since his father arrived, Martin had been bitter: Audrette had to be pregnant for Dr Gérard Préau to deign to visit his son. There was also a medical conference that the cardiologist attended each year, pencilling in time in his schedule for a lunch with his son. Rarely would he show him any affection. He hadn't been particularly encouraging about his son coming back to join him in Canada in the fifteen years since he decided to leave his mother. Nor had he prevented him from going back to France eight years later. His son embarrassed him. Dr Gérard Préau was much more affectionate with his other children, those Madelyn had given him, the Quebecois medical secretary he had met after his divorce. Something didn't click with Martin. His father had however taught him to tie his shoelaces and how to drive while perched on his father's knees. But the two had taken part in a stubborn cold war, using obsolete weapons, ignoring the origin of the conflict. No doubt he hadn't been aware of it, but was his father, deep down, waiting for the day when his son would start talking to ghosts? Even if that did turn out to be true, didn't they have some secrets to share?

Martin went to the fireplace.

'Why didn't you tell me anything about this before?' he said with a sigh.

'Because your mother was still in this world, and that wasn't her truth.'

'But still, I could have understood that ...'

'You would have ended up talking to her about it some day, Martin, and that would have hurt her no end. Do you have any idea what she endured all those years? Being abandoned by her mother – is there anything more devastating for a child?'

The poker glowed amid the flames. Martin's father used it to ensure that no bit of wood went untouched by their tongues, adding in twigs.

'My uncle didn't know what to do with her any more. She was regularly expelled from the private schools he sent her to. She finally quietened down as a teenager. She stopped talking to her mother but didn't break from her ... her fantasy.'

Satisfied, he leaned the poker back in its stand and put the Plexiglas fireguard back in place.

'Elsa was eccentric,' he said fondly. 'Charmingly, deliciously eccentric. That's what made her fascinating, and so different from the others ... Your mother saw things that we couldn't even imagine, things that reassured her. For her, there was no divide between the real and the unreal. If your grandmother came to speak to her at night, she would give her a sneaky little sign on a train platform or do a little dance move in the attic, and that was entirely normal, because she was alive somewhere, on the arm of a handsome adventurer.'

The old man stood, making his knees crack.

'Elsa was a great beauty and had a rare mind,' he said.

Then he sat down on the sofa and, with an affectionate gesture, invited his son to join him.

'You know, Martin, when you were born, it was the best day of her life. And for me, too. I was so proud of having married that woman. But how to forgive her for Bastien ... your little gent.'

Martin sat down next to his father.

Dr Gérard Préau put a hand on his son's knee.

A sweet warmth filled his eyes.

The fire emblazoned the last of the twigs.

Sleep, Bastien, sleep tight.
Granny Elsa is watching over you.
I won't let them make you suffer
like they made my poor mother suffer.
They won't get you with a needle like they did
to my father, like they do to animals.
I won't let them give you any more injections
of that rotten stuff in your blood that makes you ill
and makes you vomit, my Bastien.
You'll never be part of something bad.
I won't leave you.
I'll stop them from getting to you.
I'll always be by your side.
You'll never be cold again.
Sleep tight, my little kitten.
Granny Elsa's watching over you.

Acknowledgements

This work was created thanks to the patience and support of the people around me and whom I love biggest and best, as my son would say: my husband, my children, my friends. I would like to thank in particular my friend and doctor Françoise Brélivet-Iscache – my very own Martin! – who could single-handedly take on the job of GP in Seine-Saint-Denis any day. Thanks also to police Captain Olivier Martin, Sergeant Pascal Delannoy and Mrs Alexandra Depauile, social worker, who occupied a post similar to that of Valérie Tremblay for a time at the Gagny police station. All three do remarkable work with a marginalised community in which violence against women prevails. May they continue to do their work in the best possible conditions. Thank you to Jean-Marc Souvira for weighing in on my prose and removing the last niggling doubts of a worried author. And to my lovely neighbours – may they forgive me for drawing inspiration from their garden. Now that J.–B. Pouy has seen right through me in revealing my dishonest and perverse nature, it'll be more than a little tricky to get them to come over for tea.

It would be unfair not to mention the composers who through the emotional force of their film scores started me on the right note and gave me the tone of the characters and the events in this book. Elsa Préau owes a lot to Alexandre Desplat (*Benjamin Button*, *The Queen*, *Afterwards*), Gabriel Yard (*1408*) and James Newton Howard (*The Interpreter*, *Snow Falling on Cedars*, *The Sixth Sense*). The melancholy and the internal clash of feelings in Martin's character were sketched out listening to the music of Terence Blanchard (*Inside Man*), Thomas Newman (*Cinderella Man*) and Deborah Lurie (*An Unfinished Life*), not forgetting Erik Satie, whose music Elsa Préau uses to build bridges.

This novel was born on a table at the Salon du Livre in April 2009, a Sunday, at the end of the afternoon. I recounted what I knew of my story without knowing its true ending to Céline Thoulouze. It took a good three-quarters of an hour, until the Salon was closing – they had to throw us out! It was thanks to Céline that this book exists. And as I would never have met Céline without Nicolas Watrin and Anne-Julie Bémont-Lelièvre, thanks to them.